In the
Firing Line

In the Firing Line

Craig Rennie

CF4•K

For Dad,
who continues to inspire.

10 9 8 7 6 5 4 3 2 1
© Copyright 2011 Craig Rennie
ISBN: 978-1-84550-720-6

Published in 2011 by
Christian Focus Publications,
Geanies House, Fearn,
Ross-shire, IV20 1TW,
Great Britain.

www.christianfocus.com
email: info@christianfocus.com

Cover design by Daniel van Straaten
Cover illustration by Jonathan Williams
Printed and bound by Nørhaven, Denmark

Contents

Twelve Yards

Suddenly it all seemed so impossible. In Doug's mind the ball was a lead weight, an immovable object destined to end up anywhere but the back of the net. Running through his head were past failures – the penalties he'd missed for club and country; the day he lost his side the Scottish schools' cup final. He glanced up at the goalkeeper. When had the man between the posts transformed into such a mountainous figure? He must be at least six foot five inches, bigger maybe.

Doug's pulse quickened as he took a step back from the ball and waited for the whistle. If he missed now, he could well seal his place on the transfer list, not to mention his side's exit from the prestigious Euro League.

How had it come to this? Only one year before, Scotland's dazzling striker Doug Mackay had been the hottest property in football. An unbelievable performance in the World Cup had seen him named World Footballer of the Year at a star studded ceremony in Spain, where he stood shoulder to shoulder with his football heroes as he accepted the highest honour in the game.

Sponsorship deals, magazine covers, press conferences, transfer offers; they all came thick and fast for Doug – the Dalkirk Albion boot boy turned megastar.

After the drama of the World Cup, it became instantly obvious that Doug wouldn't be staying at Dalkirk much longer. As if his performances on the field hadn't boosted his profile enough, his role in uncovering a plot to overthrow the government of the host country had catapulted him straight to the centre of a worldwide news frenzy.

Dalkirk could name their price. Clubs from all over Europe clamoured for Doug's signature, desperately trying to convince him that a man of his talents belonged with them. In the end, it was the London club Middlewood that had their bid accepted by Dalkirk. Nobody was surprised.

The proud London club had been a sleeping giant for years, but suddenly found themselves revived after a takeover by a consortium of wealthy local businessmen. It was the stuff of dreams for Middlewood fans. Overnight they became the team to beat.

The world's greatest players were promptly snapped up, with millions of pounds being splashed around like pennies. Money was no object as Middlewood's charismatic manager Roberto Hernandez weaved together a dream team that could compete with – and destroy – the best.

Despite the galaxy of stars already signed up by Middlewood, Doug's transfer had been big news. His meteoric rise to fame from humble beginnings and stunning form at the World Cup made sure of that. On the day he posed for photos in his Middlewood shirt, a London newspaper had declared: 'Miracle Man Finally Signs'. Doug's constant willingness to share his faith in God meant articles about him more often than not had some sort of reference to his being a Christian. Sometimes they were kind, sometimes they were not. But Doug had learned to ignore the papers as much as possible and just try to focus on getting on with his job. The future looked perfect. All Doug had to do was keep turning in the type of performances that came to him so naturally, and everything would be fine. But that was the problem. Within weeks of arriving at Middlewood, things had taken a turn for the worse.

Doug's debut had naturally attracted a great deal of attention, and a full house awaited him and his team-mates as he stepped onto the lush turf at Middlewood's brand new Standbury Lane stadium for the first time.

The roar of 70,000 expectant fans had sent shivers down his spine as the whistle blew for kick-off, reminding him that anything less than victory and success was now unacceptable.

As the game progressed Doug began to worry. He had played alongside the world's greatest players before, but with each minute that passed he began to suffer from a growing sense of apprehension. In the past, it felt like he had always been fighting for the underdogs and defying the odds. But, suddenly, with so much weight of expectation on his shoulders, Doug was struggling to find his touch and even spurned two excellent chances to put the ball in the back of the net. He was substituted with twenty-five minutes still to play, and couldn't help but think his debut had been a disaster.

In the weeks that followed things hadn't improved. Average performances in domestic and European competitions saw Doug drop to the bench on a more permanent basis, with Italian international Luca Tavarno replacing him up front.

No matter how hard he tried, he just couldn't recapture the form that had prompted Middlewood to sign him, and with each game that passed Doug found it harder and harder to stay in a positive frame of mind, his thoughts often drifting to happier times playing a starring role for Dalkirk.

By the end of November, and despite Doug's form, Middlewood were riding high in the league and were building a healthy lead over their nearest challengers. But in their European games things hadn't quite been going to plan.

Draws in their first two matches and a shock defeat in their third meant the historic club now faced a huge task just to qualify from their group and claim a place in the last sixteen of the Euro League competition. Nobody could believe how badly they were struggling, especially as Middlewood were the reigning champions in the tournament, but it was widely assumed things would be put right before long.

For Doug, the situation was especially depressing, as a couple of bad misses in the first two group games had cost his team dear, and although he wasn't the only player who had failed to live up to his reputation on the big stage, he was taking more than his fair share of the blame for the team's European woes.

It was during the final Euro League group game that Doug had been presented with a golden opportunity to turn the season around – for himself, his team-mates, and the whole club.

'Get warmed up, Doug', barked Kenny Sherlock, Middlewood's assistant manager.

The young English centre forward, Kevin Banes, had just fallen victim to a badly timed challenge by one of Middlewood's Ukrainian opponents, and to Doug's surprise he was about to take his place on the field. 'Don't look so shocked', suggested Kenny, 'We paid twenty million pounds for you.'

Doug was greeted by some muted shouts of encouragement as he stretched hurriedly in front of Middlewood's home fans. Standbury Lane had been silenced after an early goal from the pacy Ukrainian side, and despite equalising at the start of the second half, only victory would secure the London team a place in the next round of the Euro League. The atmosphere was tense as the speaker system announced Doug's arrival into the game, and with a pat on the back from his manager he stepped onto the pitch – 14 minutes to become a hero.

Within seconds Doug was involved in the action. The free kick given for the challenge on Kevin Banes was whipped into the box from out on the right wing and Doug broke free from his marker, connecting with the spinning ball as it flew at his foot. He caught it sweetly, rifling it towards the goal and forcing a spectacular save from the Ukrainians' goalkeeper who tipped the ball behind for a corner kick. 'That's more like it, Mackay! Let's have more of that!' shouted Middlewood defender and Captain Jack Thornburn as he and Doug jostled with their markers before the corner was taken. The crowd sensed a goal. They roared and chanted, raising the volume in Standbury Lane to a near deafening level.

The corner was a good one, struck with pace, and once more the ball was heading straight for Doug. He escaped his marker again, and mustering all his strength he leapt to meet the dipping ball with his head. He cranked his neck back and unleashed a powerful header that had the keeper well beaten. But just as 70,000 fans prepared to erupt, the ball slammed into the crossbar and rebounded out of the box before being cleared to safety. Doug and Middlewood had been denied by inches.

Now only ten minutes remained, but Doug's blistering introduction to the game had the crowd on their feet, believing that the impossible could still happen. The humiliation of going out of the Euro League at such an early stage was unthinkable for the Middlewood support, and they willed their team on with all their might.

As the seconds and minutes passed, however, the belief began to dwindle. The determined Ukrainian players knew a place in the next round of the cup would guarantee a huge cash boost for their club, as well as securing their status as heroes in their homeland. They packed their own half of the park, choking Middlewood's efforts and throwing themselves into every tackle as if their lives depended on it.

Suddenly, with less than a minute left to play, Middlewood found an opening. A sloppy attempt to clear the ball upfield by a Ukrainian defender created a little bit of space for Middlewood's midfield playmaker Eric Tchamba. The Cameroon international glanced up, instantly spotting a darting run from Doug on the left side of the pitch. He clipped the ball over two defenders, dropping it perfectly into the path of the onrushing Doug, who was shifting with the pace and power of a runaway freight train. A roar engulfed Standbury Lane as Doug picked up the ball at the edge of the box and drove towards the keeper. With perfect balance he took one last touch and drew his foot back, ready to pummel the ball into the back of the net and send players and fans alike into a state of euphoria. But just then, from out of nowhere, Doug was sent crashing to the ground – his opportunity gone.

Then came the roar; 'Penalty!' screamed 70,000 Londoners in unison, each and every one pointing to the penalty spot and awaiting the referee's decision. And it was an easy decision.

Doug had been savagely chopped by an opposition defender, who obviously had no doubt that his team was about to concede a devastating late goal.

A red card for the defender and a penalty for Middlewood was the only possible outcome, and with all ninety minutes played this would be the final chance for what would be a truly spectacular turnaround.

But one question was being asked. The supporters, the commentators, the thousands of people watching on television all wanted to know one thing – who was going to take this all-important penalty?

With regular penalty taker Kevin Banes off injured, would it fall to team captain Jack Thornburn to take the responsibility? It certainly appeared that way as he picked the ball up from where it lay and headed towards the penalty spot. But when he reached the spot he didn't place the ball down. Instead he kept walking, heading straight towards the man he felt should be given the task of putting the ball in the back of the net – Doug Mackay.

'This is yours,' said Jack, handing the ball to Doug. 'You're on fire tonight, mate; you won the penalty – now you can win us the game.'

The atmosphere in Standbury Lane instantly became even more tense, with supporters seemingly split down the middle over the wisdom of the team Captain's gesture. After all, this was the striker whose misses had played such a big part in getting the team into this mess in the first place.

Doug himself was in two minds, but deep down he knew what he had to do. 'Thanks, Jack,' he said, as he accepted the ball from the big defender and headed towards the box. Twelve yards – that was all that separated him from putting his terrible season behind him and completely turning things around. He had played well tonight, he knew that, but if he didn't score it would all be for nothing. In a matter of seconds he would either be a hero or a villain.

His pulse quickened as he took a step back from the ball and waited for the whistle. There was no hiding place – floodlights, cameras and the eyes of football fans everywhere were on him. The whistle blew. Drawing one last breath he launched forward, striking the ball with all his power, and then watching as it sailed up, up, and over the crossbar.

Cold Call

Doug reached for the remote control and switched off the television. Watching the evening football news was not always an uplifting experience.

Tonight, a poll taken in the streets around Standbury Lane had seen eighty-six per cent of Middlewood fans agree that his signing had proved to be a big disappointment. 'He's just not got the type of class we're looking for here – he can't handle the pressure' was the blunt opinion of one angry fan interviewed – and his comments were among the more generous on offer.

Rising up from his sofa Doug stretched and walked to the window of his London apartment.

His body ached after a gruelling morning at training. His lack of first team football seemed to be having a serious effect on his overall fitness levels. 'Maybe I'm just getting old', he thought to himself.

From his window, Doug stood and watched the world pass by below. It was December, and a few weeks had come and gone since he missed the penalty that cost Middlewood a place in the second round of the Euro League.

The drama of that night had been followed by some difficult days for Doug. The anger of the Middlewood fans had been directed primarily in his direction, and, along with a couple of other expensive signings, Doug found himself out of the team for the following match.

Middlewood's manager Roberto Hernandez spoke publicly about the failure of the entire squad, not of individual players, saying that some of his new signings 'hadn't had time to gel into the team.' But, in reality, he seemed reluctant to defend Doug with any real vigour and gave the impression he was ready to use the young Scot as a scapegoat – just as long as it eased the pressure on him and appeased those who thought he should also be looking for a new job.

With each league match that passed, the situation worsened for Doug, with Middlewood's strikers Kevin Banes and Luca Tavarno knocking goals in for fun and occupying the first and second places in the top goal scorers' rankings.

Winning the league championship was now top priority for Middlewood, although their exit from the Euro League didn't mark the end of their season in non-domestic competitions. Finishing third in their Euro League group meant they would now compete in the less prestigious Continental Cup, which included teams who had finished lower down in their national leagues. As with every tournament they competed in, and despite their dramatic exit from the Euro League, Middlewood were expected to win it.

For Doug, however, none of that seemed to matter very much any more. In a few weeks the January transfer window would open, and it looked likely that Middlewood would try and recoup some of the money they had spent on buying him earlier that year. Rumours linking Doug with some top teams in Britain and abroad were constantly surfacing, but having signed a three year contract at Middlewood, it was them, and not Doug, who would have the biggest say in where he ended up.

Sitting back down, Doug reached for his Bible. In all the incredible drama and bustle of the past few months it was something he had not done often enough. His life had led him all over the world and he had experienced more highs and lows in the space of a year than most people crammed into an entire lifetime. Recently though, the difficult times he had been facing at Middlewood had really hit him hard, and in his heart he knew that only spending time in God's presence could bring him the peace he was craving and help him to put the entire situation into perspective.

Opening his Bible, Doug turned to a passage which had often helped him in the past. It was Jeremiah chapter 29, verses 11 and 12, which read: 'For surely I know the plans I have for you, says the Lord, plans for your welfare and not for harm, to give you a future with hope. Then when you call upon me and come and pray to me, I will hear you.'

Those few words helped Doug to remember that the same God who had led him through all the amazing high points in his career was still watching over him now at this low point. As Doug thought more about the passage he recalled a sermon he had heard his father preach many years before back in Scotland. He had spoken about the importance of remembering the many blessings God gives us, so that when difficult times come along, we can still be thankful and full of hope in the knowledge that God knows what is best for us.

Doug closed his eyes and offered up a simple prayer. 'Heavenly Father,' he said, 'Thank you for all the amazing blessings you have given me in my life. Thank you for the opportunities I've had to tell people about what you've done for me, and for the opportunity I have now to honour you by responding the right way in these difficult circumstances.'

As Doug continued to pray he felt a sense of peace, a feeling that the burdens of stress and worry he had been carrying around for so long were being lifted off his back.

When he opened his eyes again and looked out the window, he noticed that a few tiny flakes of snow were beginning to fall. Growing up, Doug had always loved the snow. It made even the dullest of landscapes seem spectacular, and often resulted in a day or two off school.

He smiled as he wandered over to look at the London streets once more, and decided to give his parents a call and see how everything was going back at home.

Just as he stretched across to pick up the phone, it began to ring. 'Hello' said Doug, a little surprised at the coincidental timing of the call.

It was Kenny Sherlock, Middlewood's assistant manager. 'Doug, are you busy?' he enquired. 'Eh, no, not really,' replied Doug. 'Well can you come down to the ground; we need to have a chat with you.'

Doug sensed a bit of unease in Kenny's voice. 'Is everything alright, Kenny? You sound a bit harassed.' Kenny paused for a couple of seconds before answering. 'Roberto and I just had a meeting with a couple of the directors, Doug. They've made a decision, and I'm not sure if you're going to be happy about it. We're not too happy about it ourselves, but, you know ... can you just come down as soon as possible?'

Despite Kenny's tone and the multitude of thoughts now forming in Doug's mind he felt at ease, remembering the Bible passage he had just been reading. 'No problem, Kenny, I'll be down in half an hour. And don't worry, whatever it is you have to tell me, I'm sure it can't be that bad.'

There was another long silence at the other end of the phone before Kenny spoke again. 'Oh, it's pretty bad, Doug,' he said, 'It's pretty bad.'

Relegation

By the time Doug had completed the 20 minute drive from his apartment to Standbury Lane, he had a good idea as to why he had been called in to speak to the management.

Speculation about his transfer away from Middlewood in January had been building in the national newspapers by the day. And, although no offers had been officially received, at least four top clubs had made it clear that they would be interested in offering Doug a fresh start.

Among them were Italian league leaders Mileno.

Doug's mind was racing as he locked his car and headed for the stadium's main entrance. 'How could I possibly cope in Italy?' he thought to himself, 'I can barely speak English properly, let alone Italian! But they are a big club, a huge club. Mind you,

Kenny said it was bad news, and a move to Mileno wouldn't exactly be bad, would it? Or what if a bid has been accepted from another English side? Who could it be?'

Just then, Doug stopped in his tracks and gathered his thoughts. For all he knew this meeting had nothing to do with a transfer offer. It could be about any number of things. As he stepped through the stadium doors he said a short prayer. 'Father, help me not to try and guess what the future holds, but to trust that you know what's best for me.'

Roberto Hernandez's office was an impressive sight. A cabinet in the corner was stacked full of medals and awards won at his previous club in Spain and during his time in England. He was the only manager to have won the Euro League with two different teams, and his fiery temper and in-depth knowledge of all things football related had instantly endeared him to Middlewood's success-starved fans.

Doug had been very impressed with Roberto's football philosophy and didn't hold a grudge against him for leaving him out of the team. And even though he felt the manager might have defended him more after his penalty miss, Doug understood that with so much pressure for Middlewood to win all their matches, Roberto had to make big decisions every week to keep the club's supporters, and millionaire owners, happy.

Stepping into the office, Doug was invited by Roberto to have a seat. Kenny Sherlock was there too, a look of quiet concern and exasperation on his face.

'How are you today, Doug?' enquired Roberto, his attention apparently more focused on finding some paperwork on his desk than on hearing Doug's response. 'I'm fine thanks,' replied Doug, 'Although I must admit, I'm quite curious as to why I'm here. Is there some kind of problem?'

Roberto paused, glanced up at Doug, then looked round at Kenny before letting out a sigh. 'Doug, as Kenny told you on the phone, we had a meeting with some of the club's directors today. They've asked us to speak to you and a few of the other players about the possibility of going out on loan to another team for the rest of the season.'

There was a short silence in the office. Inside, Doug's instant reaction was one of relief and excitement. What was so bad about going out on loan? It could mean a chance at first team football again, and would leave the door open for a return to the Middlewood team the following season. But before he could speak, Roberto started up again. 'The thing is though, Doug, the owners have a lot of power at the club – a big say in what happens, you know? I mean, without their money for new players we would be nowhere. Do you understand?'

Doug leaned forward, a look of confusion on his face. 'To be honest, Roberto, I don't really understand at all. What is it you're trying to say?'

Kenny butted in, determined to put things more plainly than Roberto was managing to. 'Doug, what the owners say, goes. If they tell us to loan you out, we don't really have a choice in the matter, and unless you can afford to buy out your contract, neither do you.'

Beginning to get a little restless, Doug again attempted to get to the heart of the issue. 'I understand all that', he said, 'I realise I'm under contract, but what I don't understand is, what's so terrible about going out on loan? It actually sounds like it could be a good solution right now.'

Kenny and the manager exchanged another knowing glance before Roberto finally put things in plain terms. 'You're right, Doug, going out on loan could be a good solution,' he said. 'The problem is, they want to loan you out to Bromfield – in the First Division.'

Another silence engulfed the manager's office. Doug couldn't believe what he was hearing. At the absolute worst he had thought he could end up at a team in the bottom half of the Premier League, or have to travel overseas to a good European side. But Bromfield? The First Division?

'You see, Doug,' said Kenny, breaking the silence, 'one of the directors is good friends with the Bromfield chairman. It would appear he owes him a big favour because he's also looking to loan them three other players who are out of the first team just now. Just between us, Doug, we're not happy about it. We know things haven't been going well for you so far, but we know what you're capable of. We tried to tell them we wanted to hold onto you, but they wouldn't hear it. Our hands are tied, Doug.'

For a brief moment, Doug's pride got the better of him. He pleaded with the two men, 'You need to speak to them again. I mean, I'm the World Footballer of the Year! I can't play in the First Division – especially for a team like Bromfield. They aren't even a decent First Division side! It's humiliating!'

Roberto stretched his arms out, striking a pose of resignation. 'We know all this, Doug. We can't understand it either and it's embarrassing for us too. The press will be all over it and it's going to look like Kenny and I have no say in football matters. We pleaded with them, but they have made a decision, and unless you want to sit on the sidelines for the next two and a half years it seems like your only option is to go.'

Doug could see that the two men weren't enjoying having to tell him the news, and as he began to calm down he felt bad for making their job harder. 'All right,' he said, 'if that's what they've decided then I'll go with it. I'm sure it will work out for the best.'

Kenny smiled in appreciation of Doug's decision. 'Thanks, Doug, I hope the rest of them take it as well as you.'

And with that, the meeting was over. Doug began walking back to his car, dazed after what he had just been told. His head felt light as he imagined the prospect of being forced to take what seemed like such a humiliating backward step in his career. Just then, as his heart began to sink he remembered again what he had read that morning, 'For surely I know the plans I have for you, says the Lord, plans for your welfare and not for harm, to give you a future with hope.'

A future with hope. How dearly Doug would come to cling to that promise in the weeks and months ahead.

Welcome to the First Division

The industrial city of Bromfield was exactly 166 miles north of London – a mere three hours drive from the nation's capital city.

But as Doug and his three Middlewood team-mates arrived for their first day of training at their new club, they were all pretty convinced they had landed on a different planet.

Gone were the immaculate facilities they had become so accustomed to at Standbury Lane – the cavernous gym, the one-to-one attention of fitness experts, the plush surroundings of the club's multi-million pound football academy. All were just a distant memory now.

Unlike some of their First Division rivals, Bromfield FC had failed to invest any significant money in their ground over the years. The sparse changing rooms and battered advertising boards reminded Doug of Brickwell Stadium, home of his first club, Dalkirk Albion – although at least at Dalkirk the groundsman had given the turnstiles a fresh coat of paint from time to time.

As predicted, the news that four Middlewood stars would be leaving the club to ply their trade in the First Division for the rest of the season had been greeted with near hysteria by football fans and some sections of the press.

It was a story that seemed too outrageous to be true, and one that had an infinite number of angles to explore. What had these four players done to deserve such a humiliating fate? How would they survive amid the hard-hitting football played in the lower league? And could Bromfield surge up the table and challenge for the title despite being over 30 points behind the leaders? The list of questions went on and on.

The official reason, according to the Middlewood directors, was rather simpler than most people wanted to believe. A statement issued by the club had only said; 'Following an approach by First Division side Bromfield FC, it has been agreed that Middlewood players Yuri Dvorchek, Keith Davis, Hicham Morocci and Doug Mackay will go on loan to the club until the end of the season. While we acknowledge the unusual nature of this arrangement, we believe these four players will benefit from a fresh challenge and the door will remain open for all of them to return to the side next season. We will also be willing to listen to any transfer offers made for these players during their time at Bromfield FC.'

It was a reason that left a great deal to the imagination, and the press didn't take long to jump to the conclusion that Middlewood chief executive Eddie Craven was merely off-loading some unwanted players to help out his old golfing partner and Bromfield chairman David Eaves.

As far as Doug was concerned, the reason all this had happened was no longer very important. And, despite receiving at least two calls every day from his agent, Ally Fairns, to reassure him that a host of clubs were waiting to snap him up in the January transfer window, Doug was so tired of the whole thing he just wanted to forget about it and get on with playing some football – no matter who it was for.

A brief visit home in the middle of the whole affair had given him time to speak with his parents and reaffirm in his mind that however bad things might seem, the whole situation was simply another opportunity to honour God.

Prior to their first morning of training at their new home, Bromfield manager Clive Carswell gathered Doug and his fellow Middlewood team-mates around to introduce them to the rest of the squad. With so much attention now focused on his team's progress for the rest of the season, and the obvious tension in the air as some of his first-team regulars prepared to sit on the bench for the next five months, the manager knew he was going to have his work cut out to keep everyone in the dressing room happy.

'Right guys, listen up', he started, 'Unless you haven't had your newspaper delivered for the last five years, or go shopping with the missus instead of watching World Cup finals and Euro League matches, you probably already know who these four men are. This week alone I've heard them described as 'superstars', 'football royalty', 'multi-millionaires' and 'golden boys'. Well, I don't know about any of that. But I do know one thing they definitely are – Bromfield FC players.'

Doug felt a little awkward as the speech unfolded, but he was glad the manager was trying to address certain issues before they even reared their head.

Carswell continued: 'If I'm being honest, I don't really understand how they ended up here today, and I'm sure we've all got our own ideas about that. But none of that matters now, lads. For the rest of this season we all have to pull together and do the best for this club. We can't be split down the middle. Other teams are going to up their game against us now, and every single one of us has a part to play in trying to get to the play-offs. So if there is any feeling that you don't want these guys here – for whatever reason – just drop it now. There isn't a single player here who won't benefit from finishing higher up the league – so let's just get on with it.'

It was a noble attempt by the manager to bring the players together in an unusual situation, but as training got underway it was clear that much of it had fallen on deaf ears.

A number of Bromfield players obviously felt this final training session before Saturday's match was their only chance to show that they deserved to keep their place in the team in favour of one of Middlewood's on-loan stars.

During a fast-paced and aggressive training session some hard tackles and harsh words were exchanged, with Doug attracting the unwanted attentions of the current Bromfield number 10, Rob Barkly. The club's top scorer so far that season, Barkly clearly had it in his head that his place in the team was about to be snatched from him despite doing nothing wrong. Doug could understand Rob's frustrations, but he was having more trouble understanding the constant kicks he was being forced to take during what should have been a routine training match. He was also finding it hard to bite his tongue as the youngster tried to put Doug off his game by quietly reminding him of his crucial penalty miss in the Euro League whenever there was a break in play.

By the end of the session Doug was the worse for wear, nursing a strained calf muscle with an ice pack. But despite being tempted to give Rob a taste of his own medicine during the training game, Doug saw an opportunity to show God's love and respond in a way the young Bromfield forward was probably not used to seeing in the heat of a football match. Instead of lashing out or answering back when Rob targeted him, Doug just got on with the game, even offering the striker a pat on the back and a handshake when it was all over. And, even though the handshake was only reluctantly accepted, Doug could see Rob was surprised by the gesture.

Unfortunately, Doug's ability to keep a lid on his frustrations was not shared by fellow Middlewood player Yuri Dvorchek. Like Doug, the big Ukrainian had suffered some unreasonable knocks in the training game, but unlike the mild-mannered Scotsman, Yuri had let his fists fly following one particularly late tackle. The brawl was quickly broken up, but somehow the press got wind of the incident and were all too eager to report on what they described as 'Training Ground Chaos'. As was often the case, it was an exaggeration, but it did serve to achieve the almost impossible task of further fuelling the hype ahead of Saturday's game between Bromfield and Southfield.

When Saturday did arrive, Doug found himself in a position that had become all-to-familiar this season – on the bench.

Unlike at Middlewood, however, his place in the dugout for this game was nothing to do with form, and everything to do with the kicks he had taken two days earlier in training. 'Guess Rob got his wish after all', thought Doug to himself, as he took a seat at the side of the park.

Not surprisingly, the game was a sell-out. In fact, it had been a sell-out for days, with Bromfield fans queuing for hours to secure tickets for a match that would now be shown live on satellite television. Although he would never have admitted it, the truth was that the majority of the 22,000 people there that day had come to see Doug.

His three Middlewood team-mates had certainly achieved their fair share in the game, but couldn't claim to have scaled the dizzy heights reached by him during his career so far.

As he jogged onto the turf to warm up before the game, a standing ovation and chants of 'Doug Mackay, red and white!' swept across the ground to mark the first appearance of Doug in the Bromfield colours.

Half an hour later, the ground was significantly quieter as Southfield raced into a deserved lead. A slack pass by Yuri Dvorchek in the middle of the park provided all the space necessary for the visitors to get in behind the defence and slot the ball into the net. As Southfield striker Kelvin Jones celebrated, he put both hands to his ears, as if to ask the home support why they had gone so quiet all of a sudden.

In truth, the answer to that question was obvious. Yuri's error prior to the goal was the most blatant indication that the three on-loan Middlewood players who were on the park were struggling to find the mental edge they would need for an average game in the fast-paced and hard-hitting First Division.

At half time the home dressing room was almost as silent as the stands of Bromfield's Old Mayfield stadium. Clive Carswell's attempts to rouse his team seemed futile as some of his players began to realise that having three international stars in your team didn't entitle you to win every game you played, while the pressure of appearing before an expectant sell-out crowd and a massive TV audience was clearly getting to others.

Within minutes of the second half restarting, Southfield had scored again and the Bromfield fans started getting restless. Their hopes that another indifferent season was about to be turned upside down by the arrival of their new players suddenly seemed sorely unfounded, and with the Southfield support making sure they couldn't forget the score line, Bromfield's faithful fans began shouting for an appearance from the one man who might yet brighten their afternoon.

'We want Doug Mackay, we want Doug Mackay!' came the shout from the stands, and within a few seconds the call was deafening.

Desperate to salvage something from the game, Clive Carswell turned to the man in demand. 'How's the leg, Doug, will it hold out the last half hour?'

Clive's question was posed in such a way that Doug already knew the answer the manager was looking for. 'It's fine,' said Doug 'I've played through worse.'

Moments later the fourth official held aloft the electronic board that heralded the moment football fans everywhere had been waiting for.

Number 24, Doug Mackay, was about to take the field. As expected, Doug would replace Rob Barkly. As the young striker came off the pitch he passed Doug with his head down, refusing to shake his hand. It was a gesture that prompted loud booing from the home support, but one that Doug didn't pay much attention to – he had bigger things to worry about.

From the bench he had been watching the game closely. Despite the apparent failure of his Middlewood team-mates to make an impact thus far, Doug could see that all they were lacking was the ability to make decisions a split second earlier. With so much hype surrounding today's game, Southfield were rising to the occasion and doing an excellent job of making sure Bromfield's new additions had absolutely no time to dwell on the ball. If Doug was going to make an impact, he'd have to think fast.

His first opportunity arose almost immediately when the ball broke to him 30 yards from goal. A huge roar from the crowd greeted his first touch, but before he could even pass it on he found himself on the ground. A hard tackle from Southfield defender Lee Taylor reinforced to Doug just how quickly he would have to think if he was going to make any mark on the game whatsoever. 'Welcome to the First Division,' sneered Taylor, as Doug pulled himself back to his feet.

The free kick that resulted from the tackle was at an awkward angle, but with time running out and the crowd calling for an effort on goal, Doug decided it was worth a shot. Placing the ball and looking up he could see the Southfield keeper had taken up a bad position and that the defensive wall was struggling to organise itself. The second the referee blew his whistle Doug unleashed a thunderous strike that found its way through the ramshackle Southfield rearguard and left the goalie scrambling across his line. From the moment the ball left Doug's foot it was clear there was only one place it was headed – right into the back of the net. Within minutes, Doug's introduction had had the desired effect. As he jogged back to his own half he caught the eye of Lee Taylor, who had given the foul away. 'It's nice to be here!' said Doug with a smile as he passed the defender. A polite nod from the Southfield player indicated he could take a joke.

Now Bromfield were in the mood. The sense of anticipation in the crowd seemed to be absorbed by the players, who were suddenly winning tackles they might have lost earlier in the game. Even Doug's frustrated team-mates from Middlewood now looked like they fancied it. And it was thanks to the skill and craft of one of them – Hicham Morocci – that Doug was presented with an opportunity to score a second goal 10 minutes after his first. Collecting a pass out near the left touchline, Morocci knocked the ball past the Southfield fullback and whipped an inch-perfect cross towards Doug's head. The pace and accuracy of the ball made Doug's job easy, and when his bullet header flew into the Southfield goal, the noise inside Old Mayfield was deafening.

Southfield were all over the place now, and despite their best efforts they couldn't seem to clear the ball from their own half.

Not ready to settle for a draw, the Bromfield fans seemed convinced their resurgent side could go on to get a winning goal. They were still chanting Doug's name when he picked up a loose ball right inside the centre circle with five minutes left to play. Sidestepping one lunging challenge he drove forward into the Southfield half, twisting inside another defender and playing the ball out wide to Morocci. The little winger wasted no time in heading for the by-line and cutting back another dangerous cross. This time the ball fell to Bromfield's Daryl Thomas, who directed a neat side-footed shot into the far corner of the goal to put his side 3-2 up.

The scenes of jubilation inside Old Mayfield were exceptional when the referee eventually blew his final whistle, and the continuous chanting of Doug's name made it perfectly clear who they thought was responsible for the dramatic turnaround in the game.

For Doug personally, the game had been a great way of putting the last few weeks behind him. It just felt good to be playing again after so much drama off the field.

As he left the park Doug was met in the tunnel by his charismatic agent and friend Ally Fairns. 'Well played, my son! At this rate you'll be making a name for yourself in no time!' laughed Ally. 'Very funny', replied Doug, who was confused as to why Ally had sought him out so soon after the final whistle.

'Is this important?' joked Doug, 'I've got press conferences to attend you know!'

'I know, I know' said Ally smiling, 'But that'll have to wait. I had a call from a contact in Italy today, Doug. It looks like your heroic stay here at Bromfield could be a short one. Mileno are getting ready to make a bid for you in January, and if Middlewood are true to their word they should accept it.'

Doug was stunned. As if his afternoon hadn't been dramatic enough, he was now faced with the news that he could be moving to Italy in a matter of weeks and playing for one of the World's top clubs again. It was all too much to take in at once.

'So, what do you reckon, Doug?' asked Ally, snapping the weary striker from out of his daydream. Doug looked down at his aching calf muscle. Adrenalin had helped him through the game without too much trouble, but it looked like he would pay for his bravery in the morning. 'I reckon I'd better get some ice on this', replied Doug.

'Good idea', said Ally, 'Mileno can wait.'

Money Matters

In the weeks that followed Doug's spectacular Bromfield debut, the speculation that he would indeed be joining Italian league leaders Mileno spread like wildfire.

But while the Italian club made no secret of their admiration for the star striker, those with control over his contract at Middlewood were being less up-front about the situation.

As newspapers, radio phone-ins and sports news bulletins regularly returned to the subject of where Doug would be playing his football for the rest of the season, the owners of Middlewood would only go as far as saying they would consider any transfer offer if the 'price was right'.

On the park, Doug continued in the rich vein of form that had seen him make such an impact in his first game at Bromfield. Three weeks had passed since he first took the pitch at Old Mayfield stadium, and despite the frustrations of being forced to play at a level well below what he was used to, Doug had every intention of maintaining the right attitude for as long as he was at the club.

In the two games following Bromfield's win over Southfield, Doug had netted another four goals – a hat-trick against local rivals Shellfield United and another spectacular free kick in a 1-0 win over fourth placed side Devonvale. Nine points from three games had seen Bromfield jump up six places in the league table, much to the delight of the club's enthusiastic supporters – thousands of whom had already taken it upon themselves to have the name 'Mackay' printed proudly on the back of their red and white shirts.

While he appreciated the generous support from the fans and enjoyed helping Bromfield in their bid to reach the Premier League, Doug's thoughts often turned to the possibility of taking the next step in his career. With Mileno almost certain to make an offer for him in the next couple of weeks, Doug found it hard not to get excited about the prospect of moving to Italy. At first the idea had scared him, but before long his sense of adventure convinced him it would be a perfect move. The slower style of play in the Italian league, the slightly less intense glare of the media, and the chance to turn out for a huge club with a rich tradition all appealed to Doug.

On top of all that, he knew that even if he didn't want to go, it would still be a better option than plying his trade in the lower leagues for the rest of the season and maybe sitting on the Middlewood bench next year.

Finally, after days of running through every possible outcome in his head, Doug got a call from his agent, Ally. 'Hi Ally', said Doug, nervously wondering what news his friend might have about the transfer. 'Morning Doug', replied Ally, 'Have you been watching the telly today?'

The tone of Ally's voice indicated that if he had been sitting in front of his TV, Doug would already know what Ally was about to tell him. 'I'm afraid I haven't had it on all morning', said Doug, 'Why, have I missed something?'

'You could say that', replied Ally, 'It's all over the sports news – three teams have made bids for you; Mileno, Bavaria and Cataluña.'

A wildly excited Doug cut in before Ally could say anything else. 'That's great! So how much did they bid, I mean, who had their offer accepted?'

Ally let out a sigh and paused before speaking again. 'That's the problem Doug. Middlewood have rejected all three. They said they weren't good enough offers, and that with the way you've been playing for

Bromfield you're likely to be back in London next season. I'm really sorry mate.'

Doug's heart sank.

All the weeks of speculation, the dreams of starting again abroad, the prospect of playing at the highest level; all Doug's hopes and ideas seemed to be coming crashing down on top of him. And to have to find out only after Middlewood had made a public statement about it all just seemed to rub salt in the wounds.

Ally went on to explain that Mileno had made the only really serious bid – of eighteen million pounds. It was only two million pounds short of what Middlewood had paid for Doug in the first place, and everyone seemed shocked by their decision not to make so much money back on a player who wasn't even in their squad. The Italians, who had earlier claimed they would 'break the bank' to secure Doug's signature, apparently never made an improved bid after having their first one rejected.

With little will to continue the conversation, Doug said goodbye to Ally, and slumped back on to his sofa.

Before long, Doug's phone was ringing again as family and friends heard the news and got in touch to urge him to keep his chin up and to remember that God was in complete control of the situation.

Among those who called was Doug's old friend from church, Matt Ogston. Matt and his wife Isla had just returned from a two year stint as missionaries in Uganda, where they had been helping in a home that looked after orphaned children.

Doug and Matt had been friends since they were young, and had remained close despite often ending up at opposite corners of the world.

As Matt offered words of encouragement, Doug began to feel a little ashamed. Although he had always been extremely generous with his money, he earned more in one week than most people did in a whole year. Listening to Matt's account of his last few months in Africa, he was forced to ask himself if his situation was really so bad. God had blessed him with an amazing talent and an opportunity to glorify Him by simply getting out onto a football field and doing what came so naturally. Even if his career came to an end tomorrow, God would still have a plan for him – a plan to prosper him, and not to harm him.

Doug thanked Matt for calling, and thanked God for prompting him to do so just when it was most needed.

No longer feeling sorry for himself, Doug started getting together some training equipment for a trip to the gym. Bromfield were playing in the English Cup the following day, and although his mind had been elsewhere for the past week or so, Doug knew he now had to focus on continuing his good run of form on the football field.

It was a big game for the club, who had had a relatively easy path in the tournament so far, but now faced Premier League side Lancaster.

Once again, the cameras would be on Bromfield – and Doug – as the next chapter in their surreal season unfolded.

As Doug packed the last of his training gear into a bag, there was a knock on the door of his apartment. 'Must be the postman' thought Doug, who wasn't used to visitors at this time of day.

Opening the door, he was surprised to see Ally, who he had been on the phone to just an hour or so earlier. 'What are you doing here?' enquired a puzzled Doug.

'Nice to see you too!' laughed Ally, 'Mind if I come in?'

The two men headed into Doug's living room and sat down. 'So to what do I owe the pleasure of your company?' asked Doug, 'I haven't been loaned out to a non-league team now, have I?' Both men laughed, and Ally was relieved to see Doug was in good spirits despite the disappointment of the morning.

'Actually Doug, it is about some of that business earlier,' said Ally, his face taking on a rather more serious expression. 'Not long after I came off the phone to you I had a call from a friend of mine in Italy called Tony. He's been an agent for years, and moved out there a while ago because lots of the players he represents are based in the top league. He knows the Italian game inside out, and according to one of the guys he works with, Mileno didn't just make one offer for you this morning – they made two.'

A look of confusion spread across Doug's face. 'I don't understand', he said, 'Do you mean they made a lower bid before offering the eighteen million pounds?'

'No', replied Ally, eager to get to the point. 'According to Tony's source, they made a second bid after the eighteen million pounds was knocked back – a bid of twenty-two million pounds.'

Doug leaned forward in his seat, seemingly unable to take in what he was hearing. 'Twenty-two million pounds?' he said, 'But surely Middlewood would have taken it. I mean, that's a big profit on what they paid for me in the first place. Is your mate sure about this?'

'He's pretty positive, Doug. Tony said the guy who told him was extremely reliable and has been involved with Mileno for years,' replied Ally.

'But why on earth would Middlewood do that?' said Doug, 'It just doesn't make sense – and why would Mileno not have gone public about the fact that they made an improved offer?'

Ally nodded his head, as if to acknowledge that all Doug's questions were perfectly valid ones. 'Well this is where it gets worrying', replied Ally, 'You see, according to Tony's source, Mileno never went public on the second bid because somebody paid them not to – somebody at Middlewood.'

'What?!' exclaimed Doug, 'You mean a bribe? Surely not. Why would they do that?'

Ally shrugged his shoulders. 'I have no idea', he said, 'It raises more questions than answers, but if it is true then one thing's for sure; someone at Middlewood really doesn't want you to leave Bromfield anytime soon.'

Doug was baffled, his facial expression one of complete shock and confusion. 'So what do we do next?' he asked Ally. 'Do we go to the police, the League Association? How do we find out for sure?'

Ally held up a hand, as if to stop Doug in his tracks. 'Let's not be too hasty', he replied. 'We'll give Tony a few days and I'll make a couple of calls to find out what I can. After that we'll decide on the next step. Keep it to yourself for now though; if there isn't any truth in it then it's better not to cause a stir.'

As Doug walked Ally to the door of his flat his head was spinning. Could Middlewood's owners seriously have knocked back a huge offer from Mileno, then bribed them not to talk about it? Was he at the centre of some kind of scandal he knew nothing about?

Even by Doug's standards lately, this had been a pretty dramatic morning. Opening the door to let his friend out into the hallway, Doug thanked Ally for coming round and telling him what he knew. 'No problem', smiled Ally. 'Hopefully it'll all come to nothing, but if I go missing over the next twenty four hours you can assume I've found out something I wasn't meant to!' Ally laughed at his own joke as he waved goodbye and headed off down the hallway. Twenty-four hours later, however, the situation wouldn't seem quite so funny.

Cup Upset

As he pulled on his Bromfield shirt in the moments before the First Division side's vital English Cup clash with Lancaster, Doug did his best to clear his head.

The visit from Ally the day before had raised some serious questions about what exactly had been going on in Doug's career for the last few months.

If Middlewood really had knocked back a huge bid for him from Mileno then paid them not to talk about it, the World Footballer of the Year could be about to find himself at the centre of a very unwelcome scandal.

His mind was racing as he considered all the possible reasons for Middlewood's actions, and deep down he hoped Ally's friend Tony was wrong about everything.

Not for the first time this season, however, Doug was going to have to put life off the field out of his mind as he prepared once again for life on it. In a matter of minutes, he and his team-mates would be attempting to secure Bromfield a place in the quarter finals of the famous English Cup.

A good run in the tournament meant a great deal to the club, as the money they could bring in from a prolonged stay in the competition would have an impact long after the likely departure of Doug and Middlewood's other on-loan players.

Old Mayfield was full to capacity once again, with fans and neutrals alike keen to see just how much of a difference Doug and co. would make against Premier League opposition.

Lancaster had a reputation as a very difficult team to beat, with strong and aggressive players in almost every position, and from the moment the whistle blew to signal the start of the game it was clear they had their hearts set on English Cup glory as well.

Just like the First Division sides Doug had faced since his arrival at Bromfield, Lancaster weren't shy about putting in a hard tackle or two. Their burly defenders barged and pulled Doug at every opportunity – usually out of the referee's line of sight – and as the bruising game went on he and his team-mates became increasingly frustrated. To add to their woe, Lancaster scored a scrappy goal after half an hour, silencing the home crowd and putting themselves in pole position for a place in the next round of the cup.

'We're doing fine, lads' enthused Bromfield manager Clive Carswell in the dressing room at half-time, as he tried to rally his battered side for another hard-hitting forty-five minutes. 'As long as it's only one-nil we've got every chance', he said, 'Just keep working hard and the opportunities will present themselves. They've hardly had a shot on goal themselves; we don't deserve to be behind.'

Looking around the dressing room, Doug could see Clive's attempt to rouse his troops was having little impact. After sweeping aside so many lesser teams in recent weeks, the gruelling nature of the cup fixture and the added pressure of the media's glare seemed to be taking a heavy toll on Bromfield's players.

The team was also suffering from the absence of Yuri Dvorchek, who was unable to play having already appeared for Middlewood in the tournament earlier that season.

It was at times like this that all Doug's experience came into play. He had sat in dressing rooms at half-time during some of the biggest games any footballer could ever dream of playing in. He had seen other great players encourage their team-mates when all seemed lost, sparking a fight back when it looked like defeat was just around the corner. Usually one of the quieter players at whatever club he was at, Doug had never considered himself much of a motivational speaker. But with nobody else in the dressing room apparently about to say something rousing, he thought he'd have a go.

'Let's get out there and win this!' shouted Doug as Bromfield prepared to take the field again. 'It'll all be worth it when you're standing on the red carpet at the national stadium in a few weeks!'

And with that, Bromfield headed out for the second half. Doug chuckled to himself as he left the dressing room. 'Is that the best you can come up with?' he thought. 'What an inspiration you are, Mackay!'

Despite doubting how much of an impact his brief pep-talk had made, Doug was pleasantly surprised to see that at least a few of the Bromfield players seemed up for the battle that lay ahead before the final whistle.

Lancaster continued to play their aggressive brand of football, and seemed confident that they could hold their narrow advantage by marking Doug tightly and breaking up any rhythm Bromfield tried to establish to their play.

It was a risky strategy, however, and didn't fully take into account the star quality of Bromfield's on-loan internationalists, who had it in them to turn any game with a moment of quick thinking.

With just over twenty minutes gone in the second half, and both sides becoming more leg-weary, Lancaster paid the price for their negative approach.

A cross whipped in from the right by Bromfield's David Milton was only half cleared by an off-balance Lancaster defender, who headed the ball high into the air before it fell at the feet of Middlewood's on-loan defender Keith Davis. A low drive from the agile defender – who had only scored three previous goals in his professional career – sailed past Lancaster's sprawling goalie and took rest in the bottom right hand corner of the net.

The equalising strike sparked wild celebrations on and off the field, with Keith understandably making the most of his rare moment of goal-scoring glory.

As Lancaster prepared to restart the game, Clive Carswell decided to try and capitalise on the feel-good factor engulfing Old Mayfield. Instead of holding out for a draw and a money-spinning replay away to Lancaster, he would go all out for victory in the remaining quarter of an hour.

Taking off a midfielder he threw on Rob Barkly, the young forward who had been less than friendly to Doug since losing his place in the team following the Scotsman's arrival.

It was the first time the two had partnered each other up front, and even now, as they prepared to try and take Bromfield into the cup quarter finals, Rob was proving difficult to get along with. 'Clive wants you to drop deeper', he snapped at Doug as he jogged on to the field. 'Says he needs a goal-scorer up front.'

Rob's sarcastic instructions were met with a smile and a thumbs-up gesture from Doug, who was enjoying playing a part in Bromfield's brave fight back and retained his desire to show Rob nothing but love despite his less than endearing attitude.

The game restarted, and it instantly became clear that it wasn't just Bromfield who were ready to push for a winning goal. After 75 minutes of relatively dull football the cup tie had exploded into life, with both sides throwing caution to the wind and believing they could snatch the game.

As the play swept from end to end, Doug was presented with an opening. A quick throw-in released him on the right hand side of the Lancaster half, with only one defender standing between him and the goals. With a quick step-over and a flick of his right boot, Doug left the back-pedaling Lancaster player trailing in his wake, taking a perfectly weighted touch as he bore down on the goalkeeper.

The crowd roared him forward as he edged into the box, rising to their feet as he approached the goal and willing him to shoot before the chance was gone. But Doug had been here before, and with all the calm and poise that had earned him the accolade of World Footballer of the Year he rounded the keeper.

Then, as the jubilant Bromfield fans waited for him to slot home the winning goal, he turned to the side and cut the ball back into the path of the on-rushing Rob Barkly, who had bombed forward in support when Doug first broke free.

Shocked, but extremely grateful, Rob ran onto the loose ball, gladly accepting Doug's gift and slamming the ball into the back of the empty net. As their team-mates swarmed towards the two men, Doug put an arm around his euphoric strike partner. 'Great finish, mate', he said, 'I thought you might have just tapped that one in!'

Rob smiled and returned Doug's gesture by embracing him in front of the celebrating home fans. The young striker had become so used to putting himself first in the years since becoming a professional footballer that the thought of letting someone else have the glory before him seemed like a completely alien concept.

But as it dawned on him that all the morning papers would have him listed as the scorer of the winning goal, he realised that his treatment of Doug had been completely unjustified. 'Cheers, Doug' he beamed, 'I owe you one.'

Lancaster tried in vain to salvage a draw from the game, but it was Bromfield's day. The sense of excitement and relief that swept through Old Mayfield after the final whistle was infectious, and the quiet and downbeat dressing room of half-time was now transformed into a bustling hive of activity, with players and backroom staff shouting and patting each other on the back.

When the noise had died down and the fans had left the ground, Doug slipped out of the stadium and walked across the empty car park. It had been an afternoon full of excitement, and the perfect way to forget about the questions that loomed large over Middlewood's refusal to sell him.

As he approached his car he reached into his suit pocket and pulled out his phone. As usual, he had a few missed calls, and, as usual, they were all from Ally.

'Guess he hasn't forgotten about this transfer stuff!' thought Doug to himself as he unlocked his car and jumped in.

Settling back into his seat and turning the key in the ignition, Doug noticed something unusual. The passenger seat in his car had a dirty footprint on it – something that he was certain hadn't been there on the upholstery before the game.

He stretched down to wipe the dry dirt from the seat, furrowing his brow as he tried to figure out where it could have come from. Suddenly, his heart skipped a beat as a hand stretched from the back of his car and grabbed his arm. In a state of panic Doug spun his head round, only to see a man dressed almost entirely in black sitting behind him. He was wearing a balaclava and was holding a gun just inches from Doug's face. 'Settle down,' said the man in a deep, calm, voice. 'We need to go for a little drive.'

Safe in the Shadows

Doug's heart was pounding as he slipped his car into gear and pulled away from Old Mayfield.

The shadowy figure in the back seat had ordered him to start driving, instructing him when to turn left and right through the dimly lit roads of Bromfield.

With a gun pressed firmly to his side and panic gripping him, Doug saw little alternative but to obey his unwelcome passenger.

There was a long silence in the car before Doug eventually plucked up the courage to speak. 'What's going on here? Where are we going?' he asked, navigating the car down another empty street.

The man in the back twisted his gun against Doug's side, pushing it hard against his rib-cage. 'No questions,' replied the man. 'Just turn left here then left again. We're almost home.'

Sensing that his back-seat driver would have no hesitation in pulling the trigger if the opportunity presented itself, Doug followed the instructions, and wound the car round another corner, eventually being ordered to pull into a car park next to an imposing industrial warehouse.

'Get out,' said the man in the back seat calmly. 'And don't try anything stupid – we're not alone.'

As he stepped out of the car, Doug immediately saw what his passenger meant. About twenty yards away from where he had parked, two more men emerged from a car which was tucked away in the shadows.

As they strolled slowly towards Doug and their accomplice, the smaller of the two men started to laugh. 'Is that him?' he sneered, staring at Doug through the eye-holes in his balaclava. 'Is that all you get for twenty million pounds these days? He looks like he'd break if you even tapped him with a crowbar? You know what I mean?'

The other two men remained quiet as they all crowded round, while the smaller and more talkative of the group stepped forward and leaned close to Doug's face. 'Having fun in Division One?' he said, laughing at his own remark. Doug was breathing heavily through his nose, trying to look composed but was clearly terrified. 'You really blew that game in the Euro League, didn't you?' continued the smaller man. 'Twenty million pounds and you can't even score from 12 yards – what a waste of money! I had a bet on that game as well, you owe me a tenner!'

One of the other two men, who was clearly becoming impatient with the antics of his accomplice, stepped in. 'Right, lets get going,' he said, 'We've got all night to talk about football.'

Taking a firm grip of Doug's arms, two of the men marched him towards the car parked alongside the warehouse. As they approached it, the smaller man jogged forward and opened the car boot. 'There should be enough room in here for you!' he laughed, as the other two men began to force Doug into the boot of the vehicle.

For a moment he stiffened up and began to struggle, but within seconds he felt a sharp crack behind his right ear. The man with the gun had swung the butt of his weapon down hard on Doug's head to make it painfully clear there was no escaping. Hauling him up off the ground the men shoved Doug into the empty boot of the car, slamming it shut and coming within inches of inflicting another savage head blow in the process.

Seconds later the car roared into motion and Doug could hear the muffled voices of the men in the main body of the vehicle as he lay curled up in the pitch-black boot.

A little over two hours ago Doug had been in high spirits as he left the scene of Bromfield's hard fought English Cup win. Now he found himself beaten and bruised, forced at gunpoint into the back of a car and in a state of blind panic as he wondered where he was being taken, and what would happen when he got there.

As he fought for air in his claustrophobic surroundings he tried to say a prayer. He was struggling to form full sentences in his head, but just kept mumbling the words 'Help me, Lord' over and over as the car twisted and turned its way around the streets of Bromfield. Doug had learned a long time ago that God hears our prayers no matter where we are, or how good our command of the English language might be.

Eventually the car came to a stop. Doug waited for the boot to swing open, but it remained firmly shut, and he could still hear the voices of all three men talking as the engine continued to run. Above the muffled voices and sound of the car Doug could also make out a high-pitched beeping sound which was eventually followed by the noise of a huge engine roaring and the car rattling and rumbling for a few seconds. Moments later the car started to move again, but only for a minute or two before it finally came to a halt.

This time the boot did open, and Doug looked up to see the small man leaning over him. 'Wakey wakey!' he shouted, reaching down to grab Doug's jacket and haul him upwards.

When his eyes fully adjusted to his brighter surroundings, Doug could see he was in some kind of warehouse. A dark grey floor stretched out for 30 metres or so in front of where he was now standing, and a few dusty cardboard boxes and plastic bags were piled up at random along one wall. It looked like whoever owned the building had ceased trading a long time ago.

The only light in the dank unit was coming from a small office just behind Doug, and when he twisted his head round he could see two of the men who had escorted him leafing through some kind of folder. The small man had finally quietened down and was leaning against a wall and keeping an eye on Doug with a gun in one hand and a cigarette in the other.

Eventually the other two men left the office and signalled to Doug to come with them. The small man followed on behind.

They led Doug towards the darkest area of the warehouse floor and rounded a corner into an alcove littered with more bags and boxes. The alcove stretched back for a few metres, and Doug suddenly realised that there was somebody standing very still in the shadows.

Before he could move far enough forward to make out who it was, one of the men flicked on a torch and shone it on the face of a trembling man gagged and bound in the corner. It was Ally.

Doug felt his stomach churn as he saw his helpless friend trapped in the dark. He instinctively lurched forward to try and help him, but suffered a similar fate to the last time he had tried to break the unspoken rules of his captors. A swift punch to the stomach knocked the wind from Doug, and he doubled over, struggling to catch his breath. He was pulled upright by two of the men, who took a firm hold of him on either side to prevent him trying any more heroics.

He felt powerless as he stood staring at Ally, who looked like he had suffered much more brutal treatment than he had at the hands of the three men in black.

'All right,' said the man who had first taken Doug hostage in his car, 'Let's make this quick. Your friend is wearing a gag because he likes to talk too much. We've been listening to his phone calls and we know he likes to talk about things he doesn't know anything about, and that he's already told you more than you need to know. You understand?' The man turned to Doug as he finished his sentence. 'No, I don't understand,' replied Doug through gritted teeth, 'I don't understand at all.'

'OK then, I'll make it nice and clear,' continued the man. 'Your big mouthed mate here told you something about a payment made to an Italian football team, didn't he?'

A look of total confusion spread over Doug's face. 'Well, yes, but he didn't even know, I mean, we don't even know if it's true. What's going on here?'

'Listen' snapped the man, 'All you need to know is that you play for Bromfield FC – and every time you play you'd better play to win. If you go talking to anyone – the police, or anybody else – about illegal payments, or anything else you don't know anything about, then your little mate here is a dead man. You understand now?'

The man angled his gun under Ally's chin as he finished his sentence, emphasising his point.

Doug's head felt like it was spinning as he tried to take in what was going on. But there was no time for thinking. Before he could speak again the man had turned the gun and was pointing it in Doug's face. 'Like I said, you talk, he dies.'

Glancing over at Ally again, Doug could see his friend was desperately trying to loosen the tape around his hands. But it was no use. The small man had spotted Ally's struggle as well and put an instant stop to it by aiming a solid punch into his midriff. Once again, Doug's instincts kicked in and he tried to jump forward, and once again he was on the receiving end of a body blow himself. As he struggled to get back to his feet the three men grabbed him by the arms and legs and started to hurry back towards the car they had arrived in. This time they faced more of a struggle to bundle Doug into the boot, but before long he had been forced back in like a jack in the box.

The car started up again and began to wind its way back around the streets of Bromfield, only much faster than before. Doug's head bumped and bashed off the inside of the boot as his captors swung round corners and over potholes. Before long they were back where they had started, and Doug was hauled out of the car and pushed onto the ground of the car park where his own vehicle still sat in wait.

One last time, the man who had been hiding in the back of Doug's car outside Old Mayfield made his point. Aiming his gun at Doug he said, 'You know, you seem like a clever boy. You don't have to worry about anything – just keep playing football and keep your mouth shut and everything will be all right.'

As he turned to walk away he reached into his pocket and pulled out Doug's car keys. He threw them as far as he could from where he was standing, making sure that Doug would have to spend a long time looking for them in the dark and wouldn't be able to follow him and his two friends after they left.

After the rear lights of the car had pulled away, Doug struggled to his feet.

He knew that despite the all-too-clear warnings of the men he had to call the police. 'What other choice do I have?' reasoned Doug as he started scanning the ground for his lost keys. As he began to work out what he was going to tell the police, however, he started to panic. He didn't even know where Ally was being kept. And if the men, or whoever they were working for, had tapped Ally's phone, maybe they were listening in on his calls as well. If they knew he had called the police they might act out their threats. In his head he irrationally began to imagine the sound of sirens blaring across the city and warning the men that the police were on their way.

Tired, and terrified for the safety of his friend, Doug made up his mind – he might not be able to follow the three men, but he was going to find them.

The thought of Ally tied up alone in that warehouse was too much to take, and if there was any way of rescuing him before the night was through then he was going to find it.

Scratching around on the ground in search of his keys, Doug desperately tried to remember anything that might lead him back to the disused warehouse. The car had taken so many twists and turns as he lay in the boot that he knew he wouldn't be able to trace his way there easily.

With the minutes ticking away Doug repeated his prayer from earlier that evening, stopping this time to close his eyes and bow his head. 'Help me, Lord' he whispered before recommencing his search for the missing keys.

Suddenly it hit him – just before the car had stopped at the warehouse earlier, Doug had heard some kind of engine roaring and felt the car rattling. 'It must have been a train passing!' thought Doug to himself, 'That high pitched noise I heard was coming from a level crossing!'

With his enthusiasm renewed, Doug scoured the ground as quickly as he could. If he could find the level crossing again he would be very close to where Ally was being held hostage. Just then, there was a loud beeping noise and a flash of light from behind where he was searching. Doug pivoted round to see his car lights blinking and heard the click of the doors opening. 'How did that happen?' he said out loud, before looking at the ground again. Underneath his left knee was Doug's car key. In his frantic search he had found it in a somewhat less conventional way than he intended – kneeling on it and opening his doors in the process.

Remembering his prayer from just moments before, Doug bowed his head again and offered an equally heartfelt and simple follow up. 'Thank you, Lord', he said, before jumping to his feet and running as fast as he could towards his car.

Lost and Found

After half an hour of aimless driving, Doug was completely lost.

He had wound his way deep into the industrial outskirts of Bromfield and was beginning to wonder if he would ever be able to find a route out, let alone where Ally was being held captive.

There had still been no sighting of the level crossing that Doug believed would help lead him back to his friend, and with the time now approaching midnight the whole situation seemed hopeless.

Driving along another moonlit street Doug looked out the window in search of a clue. Wherever Ally was being kept, there was a possibility he wouldn't be there for much longer, and Doug was still being driven by the same sense of urgency he had felt whilst scouring the ground for his car keys. He had to find Ally, and he had to find him fast.

Doug turned onto another wide road lined with tall grey warehouses and lowered his window to let some fresh air into the car. Almost immediately he heard something that prompted him to pull over to the side of the road.

In the distance he could make out a low rumbling and rattling sound – like the one he had heard from the back of the car earlier, only much quieter than before.

But as he sat and listened, the sound became louder, cutting through the silent industrial area with crystal clarity. 'It's a train!' thought Doug, his heart racing faster as the sound of the engine drew nearer. If he could figure out where the train line was, he would surely be able to track down the level crossing he was looking for.

He leaned his head out of the window to try and get a clear sense of what direction the train was coming from, but he needn't have bothered. Within seconds the huge locomotive roared past the end of the very road Doug was parked on, making it perfectly clear that the rail line he had been scouring the area for was now only a couple of hundred metres away.

Doug jolted the car back into gear and headed towards the end of the road. He drove slowly and kept his lights dimmed so as not to draw attention to himself. If he was getting near to the warehouse, he certainly didn't want to be spotted.

At the end of the road, the railway line could be seen on the other side of a rusted metal fence. Another wide street ran parallel to the line and Doug knew that following the line in one direction should lead him to the level crossing he had now convinced himself existed.

He took a left turn and, after driving a short distance, his suspicions were confirmed. Up ahead, the rusty fence was being illuminated every couple of seconds by the flashing of four round orange lights. The blinking lamps were indeed part of a level crossing, and if memory served him correctly, the car he had been bundled in stopped at its final destination very shortly after going over one such crossing.

Suddenly Doug's mind started to run wild. He had been so preoccupied with tracking down this clue to Ally's whereabouts that he hadn't stopped to think what he would do if he managed to weave his way back to the abandoned warehouse. These men had guns, and if they did see him or catch him in the act of trying to free Ally they probably wouldn't be afraid to use them. And how exactly was he going to get into the building without being seen or heard?

Before any more concerns had the chance to grip Doug's wandering imagination, he drove over the level crossing and continued along the road on the other side – his car headlights now switched off instead of dimmed.

The warehouses he saw here were older than many of those on the other side of the train track, and before long the road reached a dead end. Looking back over his shoulder, Doug wondered if he had already passed the building he was looking for.

Then, as he scanned his surroundings, he caught sight of something off in the distance. Beyond the end of the road in a stretch of wasteland was a building that stood on its own – smaller than those he had driven past so far and only accessible by a well-worn dirt path that continued a short distance away from where the real road finished.

Could this be the place where Ally was being kept? It would certainly make sense if it was, thought Doug. There were no street lights to illuminate the dirt road, and with rubble, unkempt grass and bushes surrounding it on every side, it had to be one of the most secluded spots in the whole of Bromfield.

The palms of Doug's hands were sweating as he turned his car engine off and removed the key from the ignition. He wished he was at home in bed, completely free of all the problems that seemed to be following him around of late. He wanted to turn around and drive away, but the thought of saving Ally spurred him on. There was no way he could leave his friend in the hands of these cruel men – whoever they were.

Doug stepped out of his car and quietly closed the door. He would walk the short distance along the track leading up to the warehouse to avoid making any unnecessary noise. As he took his first few steps along the dark path, he staggered and almost fell completely. As he struggled to regain his balance he felt his head aching from the blow he had taken earlier in the evening. It was a timely reminder that being caught trying to free Ally would almost certainly have painful consequences.

Creeping nearer to the old building, Doug decided to skirt around the outside at a safe distance. From the shadows he would be able to crouch behind bushes and look for an indication that he had found the correct location.

His first clear sighting of the warehouse offered no clues. All he could see was a tall, dark wall with no windows or visible entry points. But after continuing cautiously on for a short time, Doug became sure he was at the right place. From his vantage point behind a wiry bush he could now see light coming from a broken window high above the ground. It was very dim, but, thought Doug, could have been escaping as a result of the light switched on in the office he had seen earlier in the night.

Squinting his eyes he looked for further clues, and quickly saw what he thought was the shape of a car parked close to the corner of the building. From where he was, he couldn't see clearly if it was the car the men had been driving earlier, but reasoned that there was no chance the signs of life from inside were the result of an industrious employee clocking into the warehouse for a late shift.

Now came the next challenge – how was Doug going to get inside?

After glancing around for any indications that he had been spotted on his approach to the building, he began to move forward. In the silence of the dark night he feared his footsteps would reverberate like gunshots on the increasingly stony ground, but he pressed on.

Eventually he came to the side of the warehouse and pushed his back firmly against it hoping to be concealed by the shadows. Now he could finally make out the details of the car parked alongside the building, confirming that it was indeed the same one he had been bundled into earlier.

Still unable to hear any voices, Doug started to move along the wall in search of some way in. The pressing desire to turn on his heels and run away as fast as he could remained strong, but the knowledge that Ally was now so close kept him going.

He passed along the wall beneath the window he had seen from the bushes, and tried to picture the inside of the warehouse. When the three men had left the office earlier that night, they had led Doug the length of the industrial unit to show him where they were keeping Ally. If he could find some way in at the far end of the building he might be able to free his friend without being spotted.

As he prepared to examine the bottom corner of the building, Doug passed the parked car. With shaking hands he knelt down and began to let down each one of the vehicle's four tyres. The hissing sound as air rushed from the tyre valves seemed deafening amid his silent surroundings, but Doug knew that doing anything that might limit the men's ability to give chase later could be invaluable.

With the car tyres now almost completely flat, he continued his search for a way in; all the time staying close to the outside wall of the warehouse and the shadows it cast.

Rounding another corner Doug saw the most obvious entry point – a door. So far it had been the only way in and out that Doug had spotted, but he felt the element of surprise demanded a better alternative than strolling straight in through the front entrance. 'If they're guarding anywhere, it'll be there,' thought Doug, continuing on his way.

He didn't have to go far, however, until he saw another possible way in. Located a little further along from the door was what looked like some kind of rubbish chute. If Doug's mental image of the inside of the building was correct, the chute would open out at the opposite end of the warehouse from the office, and would offer a more covert way in than the main door.

Aware now that he was about to embark on the most dangerous part of his rescue mission, Doug took a deep breath and started to quietly investigate the potential entry point.

He was certain he would be able to fit inside it, but had no idea if it would be sealed off at the other end. He looked inside and could see that it inclined steeply from the ground, and that there was no light coming through at the opposite end. However, despite these less than positive signs, Doug concluded he had no alternative and began to squeeze his way into the old chute.

Inside it was pitch black, and Doug tightened every muscle in his body as he tried to scale his way up the metal tube. He knew that banging his feet against the rusted surfaces would create enough noise to raise the alarm, so he crawled as slowly and silently as he could, wishing all the time he was somewhere else.

Although his glance up the rubbish chute from outside had suggested there was no light coming through at the opposite end, Doug now realised this was not the case.

As he neared the top of his makeshift entrance, he could see that it changed shape, straightening out for a couple of yards before opening into the main body of the warehouse.

The end of the chute was covered by a flimsy looking metal grill that would swing open when pushed.

Crawling nearer to the grill he could see the office at the opposite end of the warehouse. Through a window the three men were visible, and despite Doug's fears about making too much noise as he moved around the outside of the building, they seemed completely oblivious to his 'break-in' attempt.

All three of them were sitting down, and had removed the balaclavas that had made them look so threatening earlier. Although he couldn't make out distinctive facial features from behind the metal grill, Doug could see, and hear, them laughing every so often. They definitely weren't expecting company.

Reaching forward, Doug pushed the grill at the top of the rubbish chute and nudged his head out of the end a little. He looked down and saw that he was about seven feet off the ground. The only way he was going to be able to get down was by climbing out of the chute head first and trying to wedge his legs against the side of it so that he could slowly lower himself to the ground.

'Maybe I should have just used the door' thought Doug, as he imagined himself clattering to the floor and causing a disastrous crashing noise in the process.

Just as he had done at the other end of the rubbish chute, Doug took a deep breath. He knew that if he could remain silent on his way in, there was a good chance he wouldn't be spotted moving in the shadows at the bottom end of the warehouse.

Edging further forward, Doug pushed his entire upper body out of the chute, glancing up every second to see if the three men still remained in their seats. His hands were still shaking as he lowered himself down the wall, his ankles and feet fixed hard against the sides of the chute to support him. A few seconds later his hands touched the ground, and he walked his feet down the wall so as not to bring them down hard on the dusty concrete floor.

He had made it in, but now sat frozen to the spot as he stared towards the office; his heart pounding as he waited to see if his entry had gone unnoticed.

Watching from the dark, Doug still saw no signs of concern among the men in the office. His view of them was clearer now, and they looked perfectly relaxed – one of them even enjoying a cup of tea with his feet up on a desk.

Doug started to move very slowly towards where Ally had been, still keeping his eyes fixed on the office. He edged his way along inch by inch and was now just a matter of feet away from his friend. Pausing again, Doug fixed his eyes on the pitch-black alcove Ally had been in earlier, and to his huge relief could still make out the outline of someone against the wall.

He took another two cautious steps forward and whispered as quietly as he could. 'Ally, it's me. Just keep quiet, all right? I'm getting you out of here.'

For a split second a terrible thought crossed Doug's mind – 'What if this isn't Ally? What if they heard me coming and this is a trap?' But before the thought could grow into panic, his fears were put to rest.

Despite having his legs tied tightly together, Ally shuffled slightly away from the wall and close enough to Doug for the two men to see each other in the darkness. Doug couldn't help but hug his friend, before whispering to him again. 'They haven't seen me. There's a way out – we just have to be silent.' Ally nodded in response.

Working as quickly as he could without making any unnecessary noise, Doug unbound Ally's arms and legs, before slowly peeling the gag from across his mouth with his trembling hand.

Free to speak once again, Ally leaned close to Doug and whispered in his ear. 'Thank you', he said. 'I didn't think I'd be seeing you again any time soon.'

Doug nodded in acknowledgement of his friend's gratitude. 'Doug', continued Ally, 'If they see us, they'll kill us.'

'I know' whispered Doug in response. 'So let's make sure they don't.'

As quietly as he could, Doug explained to Ally how he had made it back into the building and suggested that they should both be able to climb back out the same way. Ally would climb up first before Doug followed on. Both men looked back across to the office. All three men remained in their places, still unaware of the security breach.

Sticking close to the rear wall, Doug and Ally began to creep back across to the rubbish chute under the cover of the warehouse's darkness. Before too long they were in line with their planned exit point and Doug clasped his hands to provide a kind of foot support that would make it easier for Ally to climb towards the chute. 'I'll see you out there', whispered Doug, 'Just try not to make a sound.'

Ally nodded, before putting one foot in Doug's clasped hands and reaching towards the chute. He gripped the edges of it and pulled himself up silently.

As Doug supported him he turned again towards the office, but this time he did not see the comforting sight of all three men lounging around. One of them was gone, and the other two were standing up. Widening his eyes and straining to listen for any movement, Doug suddenly realised one of the men was walking across the warehouse floor in the direction of where Ally had been. Too terrified to make a sound, Doug pushed his hands up hard to try and speed Ally along, but the sudden movement had the opposite effect; putting Ally off balance as he tried to get a firm grip on the inside of the rubbish chute.

Falling back, he made a desperate lunge for anything that would keep him upright and grabbed hold of the metal grill that flipped down over the entrance of the chute. But the old grill was too weak to support him and came crashing down along with Ally to the hard floor. The hope of a silent escape was gone.

'Hey!' Screamed the man on the factory floor, 'He's trying to get away!'

In the office, the other two men jolted into action, one of them pulling a gun from his pocket as he dashed towards the source of the noise. Hauling Ally from the floor Doug remembered the door he had seen from outside. 'Run Ally!' he yelled, pulling his friend forcefully by the arm in the direction of the exit. As they reached the door, the men were just yards behind them and Doug slammed into the exit with his shoulder, opening it with the force of his momentum and triggering a wailing security alarm that ripped through the night.

As they burst back into the open air, the noise of the alarm was drowned out by an even louder sound – gunshots.

Realising they were not fast enough to keep up with Doug and Ally, the men had opted to try and stop them by any means necessary, and as two of them jumped in their car and prepared to give chase, the other fired a series of potshots in the dark. But his hand was not steady, and in the frantic confusion of the situation he only succeeded in peppering the ground around them with badly aimed bullets.

Sprinting breathlessly back along the dirt track, Doug and Ally made it to Doug's car and leapt in. Behind them they could hear the sound of the men's car engine starting up. Trying to compose himself Doug started the car and slammed it into reverse, before spinning round and speeding back in the direction of the level crossing.

Suddenly there was a loud smash and the back window of Doug's car shattered as a bullet ripped clean through it and lodged in

the dashboard between the two escapees.
For a split second, Doug lost control of the
vehicle, veering all over the road in a state
of panic. But then he was off again, winding
his way back through the industrial estates
of Bromfield with his foot pressed firmly to the
accelerator.

Shaken up and barely able to catch his
breath, Ally turned his head cautiously and
looked through the hole where the back
window used to be. 'I can't see their car,' he
said, 'Why aren't they following us?'

Doug glanced in his rear view mirror as if
to confirm Ally's information. 'Flat tyres', he
said, as he swerved round a sharp bend and
sped off in search of the police station.

The Twelfth Man

The young constable at the reception desk in Bromfield Police Station had nearly choked on his coffee and cake when Doug walked through the door.

It wasn't every day that the World Footballer of the Year strolled into the station in the early hours of the morning to report being caught up in kidnappings and shoot-outs immediately after netting the winning goal in a crucial cup tie.

The sight of his favourite player accompanied by a frail-looking sidekick covered in dirt and dust, had left the officer momentarily speechless, but before too long Doug and Ally were afforded the opportunity of relaying the events of their evening to two special branch detectives in an interview room.

Thankful that their night had ended in the safe confines of the station, Doug and Ally told the detectives all that had happened, explaining that the trouble seemed to centre on Ally's phone conversation with his Italian friend Tony about an illegal payment made from Middlewood to Mileno.

Ally revealed that, like Doug, he had been abducted by the men earlier in the evening, only in his case it had happened as he set out from home to go to the cup tie at Old Mayfield.

Promising to get to the bottom of the whole affair as quickly as they could, the detectives arranged for Doug and Ally to be driven to a safe location for the time being to keep them out of harm's way. They all agreed that whoever these men were, there was a chance they might now be looking to take even more drastic action following Doug and Ally's escape.

All Doug could do now was wait. His transfer to Bromfield may still have been shrouded in mystery, but the police were looking into it and he knew that if anything illegal was going on, he was completely free from blame. Still, he couldn't stop questioning why Middlewood would be so determined to make him play in the First Division and refuse to sell him to another club for a hefty transfer fee – or, indeed, why anyone would employ such terrifying methods to prevent him or Ally from looking into the matter any further.

* * *

Three days after his visit to the police station, it was time for Doug to take to the football field once more. He and Ally were both still living outside of Bromfield in a house that was under the watchful eye of the police, and both of them were hoping it wouldn't be long until they could return to their respective homes. So far they had only told their closest friends and family about what had happened earlier in the week, and were eager that nothing would appear in the newspapers about the story to further antagonise the situation or draw even more attention to Bromfield during what was already a bizarre season.

Today's match would see Doug and his Bromfield team-mates travelling 100 miles down the motorway for a vital match against high-flying Wexvale Rovers. Wexvale had enjoyed a dream start to the season, racing six points clear of their nearest challengers before Christmas, and maintaining good form in the New Year to make sure they were still favourites for the First Division title. They had been relegated from the Premier League the season before, and clearly had every intention of making an instant return to the top flight. For Doug, the knowledge that Wexvale's 40,000 seat stadium would be full to the brim rekindled the kind of pre-match excitement he was used to feeling before the biggest of matches he had played in.

Bromfield's run of form since the arrival of Doug and his fellow Middlewood squad mates had seen them rocket up the league table – jumping from 19th to 7th over a period of just six weeks. A win against Wexvale today would put them within touching distance of the play-off places, and signal their arrival as true promotion contenders.

When he stepped out on to the pitch to start his warm up, Doug realised that, like him, both sets of fans were looking forward to this crunch game. The sound of boos directed at Doug from the home fans almost completely drowned out the raucous chants of support coming from the travelling Bromfield delegation, and it was clear that Wexvale did not relish Bromfield stealing their status as the team to beat in the league. If there was any opportunity to unsettle the northern side's star player, the Wexvale fans were not going to be slow in taking it.

When the referee blew his whistle to signal the start of the match, Wexvale's speedy winger Kyle Robertson quickly set the tone for what would follow. Sprinting to reach a loose ball before Bromfield's Hicham Morocci, Robertson hit the ground running and slid towards the skilful midfielder with his studs up. While his high-impact challenge didn't make a lasting impression on Morocci, it earned the fired-up Robertson a yellow card and proved beyond any doubt that Wexvale had their minds firmly set on putting Bromfield in their place.

The challenge came after just twenty seconds, and succeeded in stirring both sets of fans up into a frenzied state. Like Hicham Morocci, it wasn't long before Doug was on the receiving end of some hard knocks, and every time he came within touching distance of the ball the Wexvale fans struck up with a deafening chant of 'Reject! Reject! Reject!'

After half an hour of frantic action, Wexvale carved out an opening that had everyone in the stadium on their feet. Their huge striker and former England international, Daryl Thomas, rose to meet a long ball with his head and flicked it over the last Bromfield defender to release fellow forward, Phil Hughes. Picking up the ball at full speed, Hughes dashed into the box and skilfully knocked the ball round the keeper. But before he could finish his run by slotting the ball into the empty net, he felt the tug of the goalkeeper's hand on his ankle and tumbled to the ground in a heap.

Watching from the halfway line, Doug's heart sank as he realised Bromfield had surely given away a penalty and would probably have their goalie sent off as well. And he wasn't the only one in the stadium who thought the foul merited the harshest possible treatment. The Wexvale fans waved their arms furiously and screamed for justice to be done, while the team manager Cliff Hayles and his coaching staff rushed forward from the home bench to make the same demand of the referee. Somehow though, the unbelievable happened. Instead of pointing to the penalty spot, the referee waited for the ball to roll out of play and reached into his pocket before casually producing a yellow card to wave in the direction of Hughes.

If the accusation that Hughes had taken a dive made the Wexvale fans irate, their anger paled into insignificance compared to that of their fiery striker, who reacted to the referee's decision with total disgust. Flailing wildly and shouting in the referee's face while his team mates steamed in to back him up, Hughes was shown a second yellow card as quickly as he had been shown the first and ordered to leave the field of play.

Suddenly things turned ugly. Hughes clearly wasn't ready to see his afternoon end so rapidly for no good reason, and made his way over to Bromfield keeper Tommy Bjarnason to make his feelings known. A shoving match quickly followed between the two players, and when Hughes took things too far and rammed a hand in Bjarnason's face, almost every player on the pitch bolted onto the scene – shoving, pushing and swinging fists in a display that threatened to see the match abandoned altogether.

For Doug's part, he joined a couple of the more experienced Wexvale players in trying to pull the warring sides apart and calm the situation down. When something like peace was eventually restored, the referee made what seemed like another incredibly unwise decision by singling out a second Wexvale player and showing him a red card, whilst offering nothing more than a tough word to Bromfield's worst offenders. His actions prompted more furious protesting, and the anger being directed towards the referee on the pitch had clearly spread to the stands.

A handful of Wexvale fans tried to jump onto the field of play, forcing the police to charge in and restrain them. It took a full 10 minutes for the game to resume, and the last quarter of an hour of the first half was a tense affair crammed with more shoving and barging than any two teams should indulge in over the course of a whole season.

When the less than popular referee did finally blow his whistle for half-time, he and the Bromfield players were treated to a hail of bottles and pies as they made their way down the tunnel. It was the nastiest atmosphere Doug could remember ever having played in, and he couldn't help but wish the referee had just given the penalty and consigned them to falling a goal behind.

As they sat at half-time, the Bromfield players could hear banging and shouting coming from the Wexvale dressing room further down the corridor. They were clearly wound up, and in no mood to lose after feeling they had been denied a stonewall penalty.

As the action got underway in the second half, they began to channel their anger into very positive football. Although they were now two players short, they worked hard to close down every pass Bromfield made; hassling their opponents at every opportunity and playing fast and direct football when they had the ball in their possession. Before long their determination paid off. A powerful through pass from the centre circle split the Bromfield defence and released Chris Thomas, who made no mistake in thumping the ball home from just inside the box. The celebrations of the Wexvale players and fans showed a massive sense of relief at finally getting the goal they felt they had been robbed of in the first half.

But for all their efforts, it wouldn't be long before Wexvale found themselves surrendering their slender advantage. Their hard work and running had served to release much of their frustration, but it had also left 9-man Wexvale a little short on energy. Just five minutes after they went ahead, a curling cross-field pass from Yuri Dvorchek released Hicham Morocci on the left hand side of the field. Twisting inside the Wexvale right-back he knocked a perfect pass to Doug, who gratefully dispatched the ball low into the bottom corner of the Wexvale net. As he applied the finishing touch to Morocci's pass, however, Doug felt a hard knock on the back of his left leg. In a last ditch effort to clear the ball, a Wexvale defender had slid in hard and brought Doug tumbling to the deck. Pulling himself to his feet to accept the adulation of his team-mates, Doug realised he wouldn't be able to play any further part in proceedings.

The tackle had been nasty enough to leave him with an agonising dead leg, and as he limped back up the park for the restart, he signalled to the Bromfield bench that he would have to come off. It was a painful end to a gruelling afternoon's work, but Doug could at least take some comfort in knowing he had drawn his side level.

He was replaced after 72 minutes by Rob Barkly, who took to the pitch with a message for the other players from Bromfield manager Clive Carswell. Fully confident that Wexvale were now flat out of energy, he urged his team to push for a winning goal and compound the misery of their hosts.

But his confidence was misplaced. Weary as Wexvale's nine men were, they continued to battle hard for every loose ball and even managed to muster a couple of dangerous attacks to keep Bromfield's defenders busy. When the fourth official held up his board to indicate there would only be a further two minutes of added time to play after the ninety minutes were up, some fans began to head for the exit. The drama of the first half now seemed like a distant memory as the seconds ticked away and the game fizzled out to a weary stalemate.

Suddenly though, there was a spark of action. What should have been a simple pass out of defence by a Wexvale defender turned into a golden opportunity for Bromfield when the unfortunate centre back slipped and pulled the ball into the path of Rob Barkly. Wasting no time in pouncing on the mistake, Barkly jinked through a space in the Wexvale defence and burst into the box at full speed. Determined to make amends for his nightmare error, Wexvale's weary defender had scrambled to his feet and dashed after his opportunist opponent. Just as Barkly pulled his foot back to shoot, the chasing Wexvale player made a desperate lunge and succeeded in knocking the ball out of play. It was an outstanding tackle. Knocked off balance by the challenge, Barkly hit the ground, frustrated that he had lost his last-ditch opportunity and a little embarrassed that he hadn't managed to make more of the chance. As he pulled himself to his feet however, the referee pulled one last surprise out of his hat for the travelling Bromfield support to enjoy. Running forward and giving a short sharp burst on his whistle, the official pointed to the penalty spot. For a moment he was greeted with looks of stunned confusion, but as the reality of the decision set in, and the sense of injustice stirred up in the first half resurfaced afresh, the Wexvale players, fans and coaching staff lost their heads all over again. Once again the players bolted towards the referee – surrounding him and barging him furiously as they screamed in total disbelief. For the second time in the afternoon, some irate Wexvale fans tried to get on the pitch, but were contained by the huge ring of policemen and stewards who had lined the perimeter of the playing surface in preparation for the final whistle. The team's manager, Cliff Hayles, had to be hauled back into his technical area by the fourth official as he too attempted to charge onto the pitch and share his thoughts with the referee at close quarters.

Looking on from the bench, Doug struggled to remember an afternoon like it in his illustrious career. And while he hated to see the ugly side of football rearing its head, he did have some sympathy for Wexvale – it had been a shocking decision by the referee.

As in the first half, it took a long time for things to calm down again. When they finally did, it fell to Rob Barkly to take the penalty. Whether his side deserved it or not, he had no intention of letting another good chance go to waste and sent the ball high into the top left corner of the goal. The noise of the celebrating Bromfield fans simply served to heighten the angry atmosphere, and the time added on at the end of the game to account for the protests of the Wexvale players was played out in a very unpleasant spirit. Eventually the referee put everyone out of their misery and blew for full time before being escorted from the field of play by several policemen ready to ward off the irate Wexvale players and staff. Unsurprisingly, the hail of plastic bottles that had greeted the official's exit from the pitch at half-time was repeated with even more severity as he left for his dressing room once more.

In his post-match interview half an hour later, Wexvale manager Cliff Hayles took the opportunity he had been denied earlier to share his thoughts on the referee's performance. 'I know I'll get a hefty fine for saying this, but I don't care,' he said, his cheeks still flushed with rage. 'If that guy ever referees another professional game there should be some kind of investigation. We've just been robbed in our biggest game of the season and it's not right. People pay good money to watch football and they have to put up with shambolic decisions like that. Honestly, someone should take a good look at a tape of our game today because everyone in the stadium knew we should have had a penalty and they shouldn't have.'

He paused for a brief second as if carefully considering his next comment, but couldn't refrain from blurting it out. 'If you ask me,' he said, in a quieter and more serious tone, 'that was nothing but a fix.'

Every Last Word

Bad refereeing performances in football were nothing new, and within a few days the farcical officiating witnessed in Bromfield's undeserved win over Wexvale was yesterday's news. The governing body of the league had given an opportunity for the referee in question to speak publicly about his performance – an opportunity he used to apologise for what he admitted to be 'bad mistakes' and acknowledge that he 'fully understood' the league's decision to place him in charge of lower league matches for the remainder of the season. As was standard in such incidents, Wexvale manager Cliff Hayles was subjected to a hefty fine for what were deemed to be inappropriate post-match comments about an official who had simply had an off-day, while the club itself was also forced to cough up a sizeable sum of money for failing to control its fans during the ugly scenes that had erupted that afternoon. It was a bitter pill to swallow for the proud club, made all the more frustrating by the fact they had gone on to lose a string of subsequent matches and drop from the top of the table into the play-off positions.

The general consensus in the media had been that Bromfield's dramatic season and comparable abundance of star players had simply turned them into the division's glamour team, earning them unmerited access to the kind of generous refereeing decisions that seem to be unfairly reserved for those select clubs that already boasted significant advantages in talent over their opponents. Whatever the case, Bromfield had performed rather better than Wexvale since the controversial fixture, winning the majority of their league games by comfortable margins. Doug, suitably recovered from his minor injury, had continued his exceptional run of form by scoring no less than eleven goals along the way. The precious points earned meant that Bromfield now needed only a draw in their final game of the season to cement their spot in the league play-offs.

Unfortunately, the club hadn't enjoyed the same measure of success in the English Cup. While the injury Doug picked up against Wexvale hadn't prevented him from turning out for league duties, he had missed out on a high profile cup quarter final earned earlier in the season by merit of the hard-fought win against Premier League side Lancaster. Minus their star man and the cup-tied Yuri Dvorchek, the club had suffered a frustrating one-nil defeat to the hands of another top flight side, the industrious and well-organised Fulsham. As disappointing as the result was following the heroics of Doug and co. in the previous round, everyone at the club seemed to share a secret sense of relief that all their efforts could now be squarely focused on the league campaign. For while English Cup glory had evaded them this year, Bromfield's dream of a place in the Premier League – and one of the most dramatic turnarounds in First Division history – remained very much alive.

Down at Old Mayfield, Doug was packing the last of his kit into his bag before heading home from training. The shock of Ally's kidnapping and the surrounding incidents had become increasingly far from his mind in recent weeks, despite the fact the police still seemed no closer to delivering an answer on what had been the cause of it all and a lingering sense that whoever was behind the events could strike again. In truth, Doug had other things on his mind.

The next day he would be flying to Rome, where he was due to play a part in the ceremony crowning this year's World Footballer of the Year. As the previous winner of the award, the task of handing over this year's trophy to his successor fell to Doug. While some players had considered it a dubious honour in the past – frustrated by the fact they weren't winning it once again – Doug was humble enough to see the poignancy of the gesture.

This year however, that gesture would be a little more poignant than usual. Not only had Doug's fall from top flight football been dramatic and well-documented in the months since he received the honour, the newly-crowned recipient was none other than Middlewood's Luca Tavarno – the Italian international whose excellent form at the start of the season had effectively forced Doug out of the first team and then out of the door at the London giants.

But despite advice from some team-mates to avoid the ceremony and the attached ignominy it would surely heap on Doug, he was in no doubt that he should attend. Yes, the press would have a field day as they reported on the contrasting fortunes of the two players, yes the questions would come about whether he wished things had turned out differently and yes, there would be those asking if Doug could ever again scale the professional heights he had so recently fallen from.

But none of that mattered. As a Christian,

Doug knew well that nurturing personal pride and clamouring for public praise were not honourable qualities in the sight of God. To be Christ-like in such situations meant showing humility, treating others as you would want to be treated and living a life designed to please God and not other people. Whatever anyone said, he'd be going to Italy to hand over the award and offering his heartfelt congratulations to Luca in the process. And while many people viewed the whole situation as an intriguing coincidence, Doug's belief that God had control over all aspects of his life meant he saw this as a gift and opportunity to show a selflessness that was becoming all too rare in professional sport.

As he walked down the corridor on his way out of the stadium, Doug heard someone shout his name from one of the rooms along the way. Doubling back and glancing through a doorway, he could see it was the chairman's son, Ryan Eaves that had called to him.

'Hi Doug,' said Ryan, 'Do you have a minute?' Ryan was a friendly young man who had recently graduated with a degree in business studies before taking on a role with Bromfield. He was around the same age as Doug, and had a good rapport with the players at the club thanks to his amiable manner and genuine interest in their wellbeing. His friendliness was often seen as being in stark contrast to his dad's more dour demeanour, which meant players usually went to Eaves Jr. first when they had off-field matters to discuss.

'Oh, hi Ryan,' said Doug 'Sorry, I never saw you there on the way past. How are you?' Ryan paused for a second before answering. 'Oh, I'm all right thanks. I just had a quick question for you.' 'I'm all ears', responded Doug with a smile. Ryan tidied some papers from his desk and glanced beyond Doug into the corridor, as if to make sure nobody was loitering nearby. 'I was in touch with some friends at the World Football Organisation this morning, and I've managed to get a ticket for the awards ceremony tomorrow night. I was wondering if I might be able to tag along with you – maybe catch the same flight?' Unnerved a little by Ryan's apparent secrecy over what seemed like a simple question, Doug glanced quickly over his own shoulder before replying. 'Of course, that would be great. Ally was planning to come, but he can't make it. And I could use some company to be honest, you know, with the way the press are probably going to be and all that.' 'Yeah, that's what I thought,' said Ryan with a smile. 'If you can send me your flight details I'll see if I can arrange a ticket for the same plane.' As he finished his sentence, Ryan again cast his eyes through the open doorway as Fiona, the enigmatic tea lady, rattled by with a trolley full of glasses. 'No problem at all,' said Doug, studying Ryan's face for a second before speaking again. 'Is everything all right mate?' he queried. 'You seem a little, well, edgy, or something.' Ryan returned Doug's glance even more briefly before cracking another friendly smile. 'Sorry, yeah, everything's fine,' he said. 'Send me those flight details and we'll see if we can't make this trip a bit more worthwhile, all right?' Doug nodded and made for the door. 'Will do,' he said, wondering exactly what Ryan meant by 'worthwhile'.

Twenty-four hours later, Doug and Ryan loaded their bags into the overhead luggage racks of the plane and took their seats. Accustomed as he had become to travelling first class since mixing in the upper echelons of the football world, Doug still couldn't help but feel he didn't belong in the more luxurious section of an aircraft. As if to confirm his suspicions, a teenage boy glanced at him on his way down the aisle, before whispering to his friend with minimal subtlety, 'That's that guy that used to play for Middlewood!' Ryan couldn't help but chuckle. 'Your fame proceeds you mate,' he said, unsurprised to see that Doug was laughing himself.

Soon they were in the air, chatting about the season so far, the remaining matches that lay ahead and the exciting likelihood of a place in the play-offs. As they spoke, Ryan unfolded a newspaper and turned a page featuring an article on Doug's role in the awards ceremony that night. 'I was reading this earlier on,' said Ryan, pointing at the article. Doug leaned over to see what Ryan was referring too. 'Oh yeah, I spoke to someone from the paper yesterday after training,' said Doug. 'I'm sure they'll have plenty more to say once they have a photo of me handing over my trophy tonight!' 'Yeah, probably,' laughed Ryan, before continuing. 'Seriously though, I'm impressed with how you're handling this. Most players would have avoided something like this like the plague. There's no ego with you, Doug, you definitely practice what you preach.'

Before Doug could thank Ryan for the kind compliment, the chairman's son carried on. 'It's not just this. You've had to put up with abuse from the away fans all season, and even some of our own players at first. The way you've handled it all has really got me thinking. I'm always worried about what's best for me and how I can get ahead, but you've gone through a bit of a nightmare really, and you still seem to be thinking about how you can do the best by everyone else.'

As he spoke, Ryan didn't look at Doug, but instead fixed his gaze on a piece of paper he had been scribbling on for the last few minutes. As his words tailed off, he turned to Doug, looked at him for a second then motioned towards the bit of paper with a tilt of his head.

Furrowing his brow in confusion, Doug followed Ryan's subtle instructions and cast his eyes towards the sheet of paper resting on the fold-down table in front of his travelling companion. He stared at it for a second to find something of significance among a mess of doodles and scribbles, before eight words that Ryan had written down in capital letters suddenly grabbed his attention. They read: THERE'S BEEN FOUL PLAY AT BROMFIELD THIS SEASON.

Now even more confused, Doug immediately looked back up at Ryan, but the chairman's son again indicated that the piece of paper before him was a more appropriate source of answers. Doug glanced back down, where Ryan's hand slid aside to reveal three more words: I KNOW EVERYTHING.

Utterly baffled by the sudden turn of events, Doug could no longer remain silent. 'What's going on here?' he queried sharply, his voice hushed but betraying his state of disbelief. Now Ryan did meet his stare, nodding his head briefly as if to indicate that he realised that a much greater explanation was necessary. He raised his index finger briefly in a request for Doug's patience, then reached into his coat pocket and produced a small MP3 player. He handed the player and attached earphones to Doug, before breaking his silence. 'Listen to the third track on there, Doug,' he said, 'I think you'll find it interesting.' And with that he broke Doug's bewildered gaze and reached again for his newspaper to indicate he wouldn't be taking any further questions on the bizarre exchange that had just occurred.

Doug sat motionless for a moment and peered at Ryan, then looked down at the MP3 player in his hands. With a seemingly infinite number of confused thoughts colliding in his head, he slowly placed the headphones into his ears. Questions of whether something suspicious had been taking place at Bromfield hadn't entered his mind for some weeks now. But as he skipped to the third track on the music player, the sudden realisation that he was on the verge of discovering the whole truth behind his transfer away from Middlewood brought the unsavoury events of the year so far flooding back to his memory. He slid his thumb over the buttons of the MP3 player, skipping to the third track as Ryan had instructed and pressed 'play'.

There was a quiet buzzing sound through the earphones for a couple of seconds before a recording of Ryan's voice began to play.

'Doug,' began the recorded message,

'I'm sorry that you have to hear what I'm about to tell you this way. It's too risky to discuss out loud, so I recorded this message last night after we arranged to travel together.' There was a pause of a few more seconds on the recording before Ryan's voice started up again.

'What I'm going to tell you could be hard to believe, but please listen all the way through and don't ask any questions here. We can't talk about this in public.' Ryan's voice was audibly trembling on the recording, and as Doug cast a sideways glance at him for a brief moment, he could see his hand was shaking slightly as well as it gripped the edge of his newspaper. Determined to focus on nothing other than what he was listening to, Doug closed his eyes and allowed the rest of the recording to play out.

'You're a pawn in a game, Doug. Your transfer to Bromfield isn't as straightforward as some people would like to make out. In fact, it's far from it, and it's part of some illegal goings on that are going to have serious consequences for the people behind it. That's why it's so hard for me to tell you this – because one of the people behind it is my dad.'

Doug opened his eyes abruptly; desperate now to talk through whatever Ryan had to share face to face. But as he looked round he saw that the seat next to him was empty. Ryan must have removed himself to elsewhere on the plane in order to avoid any breaks in Doug's concentration. The recording played on.

'A few weeks ago, the police paid a visit to the club and interviewed myself and my dad about a kidnapping incident in which Ally was taken on the night of our cup match with Lancaster. The police said their visit was just a routine part of their procedures, and they seemed happy to accept our claims that we knew nothing about the incident. In my case, that was true, but I couldn't help noticing my dad seemed very uncomfortable with their presence in his office. After they interviewed us, he seemed to change. He was jumpy and agitated, and he often worked from behind closed doors after that day. Before long I started to wonder if he knew more than he had admitted.'

'I gave some thought to the season. I thought again about the fact that you and three other Middlewood players ended up at a struggling First Division side. Dad had assured me at the time that it was all simply through his friendship with Eddie Craven at Middlewood, and I accepted that. But when the police told us that Ally's kidnapping seemed to revolve around a phone call he'd had relating to an illegal payment made to a team in Italy, and there were accusations of a fix following our game with Wexvale, I felt there were too many unanswered questions to ignore.'

'I started to stay late at the stadium and trawl through old phone records, e-mails, answer machine messages – anything and everything I could think of to find some answers. And, I'm sorry to say, they weren't hard to find. Dad had been sloppy in covering his tracks, and before long I had a clear picture of what was going on.'

There was another break in the recording as Doug felt his seat bump backward slightly. Ryan had taken his place alongside him again, but simply met Doug's stare with another silent gesture designed to remind him that he had nothing to say other than what he had already committed to the recording. Doug continued to listen.

'Doug, I know you're not a betting man. Neither am I. Unfortunately, the same can't be said of my dad and some of his friends. They have more money than they know what to do with, and sadly one way they've always spent it is by gambling. That's the essence of what's been going on this season. Your presence at Bromfield is part of a huge betting scandal, Doug.'

Doug felt a wave of shock passing through his whole body as Ryan began to unravel the full extent of his findings within the walls at Old Mayfield.

'When you signed for us in January, we were in 19th place in the First Division. We had no chance of winning the league. We were miles away from the top of the table, with one of our weakest squads in years. The odds of us winning the league were around 1,000-1. That means, if someone bet ten pounds on us winning the title and we managed to do it, they'd win ten thousand pounds. Of course, that would have been impossible. Well, it would have been impossible with the team we had. But would it have been impossible with the best player in the world playing for us? Would it have been impossible if half of our side was made up of international superstars?'

'Those were the questions my dad and his friends on the board at Middlewood were asking themselves. And tragically, they couldn't resist the urge to find out. But they didn't just bet ten pounds. They bet fifty thousand pounds. I'm sure you can figure this out, Doug, but if we won the league, that means they'd win fifty million pounds. I found evidence that they placed the bets over the period of a few weeks, in lots of different locations and by lots of different means so they wouldn't get noticed. But it didn't matter how and where they did it, as long as they did it when Bromfield were lying low in the league and before we suddenly became the most talented team in the division and had the odds of us winning it significantly reduced.'

Doug put his hand to his head as utter disbelief gripped him. If what Ryan was saying on the recording was true, he had indeed been little more than a pawn in a game being played by rich men with no interest in anything other than becoming even richer. But there were still questions to be answered, and the recording had not yet come to an end.

'From what I can gather Doug, Middlewood didn't sign you with the intention of doing this. It just so happened you were on the bench when the plan was put into action. Perhaps it worked out perfectly that you weren't the kind of guy to complain and make a scene like some other players might have. Your humility and broader perspective on life and its many twists and turns meant the media attention started to shift away from the situation off the pitch and towards events on it. The only thing that could have ruined the plan was if other teams had made good offers to Middlewood for you and your team-mates in the January transfer window. If Middlewood refused to accept excellent bids for players that clearly weren't in their plans, suspicions may have been raised. As you know, some low bids by teams hoping to get you and the other players on the cheap were easily rejected, but there was another bid that couldn't be made public.'

Doug silently mouthed the word, 'Mileno.'

'When Mileno offered twenty-two million pounds, it had to be swept under the carpet, or people would know that Middlewood had some major interest in keeping you right where you were at Bromfield. Ally's friend in Italy was right; Mileno did accept money from the board at Middlewood to keep quiet about the offer they had made. I don't think they knew what was going on, but they must have been happy to take the cash and consider the matter closed. It seems corruption is almost everywhere. Ally got too close to the truth, which is why he must have been kidnapped that night. But when the police couldn't get any closer to the answer, it must have seemed to my dad and his associates that everything had blown over.'

'The final part of the equation, the thing that pushed me into finding out the truth, was our game with Wexvale. The referee was more than just bad in that game, he was crooked. There are documents that prove he accepted an illegal payment to ensure we won that game by any means necessary. As you know, Doug, we're close to the top of the table and looking good for the play-offs, but the bet would only come off if we won the league. A few weeks ago, dad and his friends wanted to make absolutely sure we got three points in what was potentially our most difficult game. They succeeded,

I suppose, but their actions there will prove to be their downfall.'

There was a final pause on the recording before Ryan came to the end of his long explanation.

'I'm sorry, Doug,' he concluded, 'I'm sorry you were dragged into this, and I'm sorry you had to find out here and now. I'm also full of regret that, when all is said and done, it is ultimately me that will be responsible if my dad goes to prison. But if there's one thing I've learned from watching you this season, Doug, it's that it's more important to do the right thing than look out for your own interests. All the evidence I gathered is with the police. When we get back to England tomorrow, this will all be over. I made this trip with you because I couldn't face being there when everything unfolded.'

There was a click and the recorded audio stopped. Doug stared off into space for a second before removing the headphones. Aware that he could say virtually nothing on the subject, he took a deep breath, turned to Ryan and quietly whispered, 'Are you sure that's all true?'

Relived that his secret had now been shared with the person it perhaps affected most, Ryan finally spoke. 'Every word, I'm afraid.' He said with a sigh. 'Every last word.'

In the Firing Line

The plane touched down in Rome at 5 pm local time, the pilot announcing that the weather in Italy was a significant improvement over the rain-soaked scene those on board had left behind in London a couple of hours earlier.

Unable to discuss the recorded audio Ryan had shared with Doug at 25,000 feet, the two men had spoken little for the remainder of the journey, exchanging only cursory pleasantries about the view, the in-flight food and the evening ahead as the plane made its descent into the famous city. It wasn't until they found some space away from the other travellers in the baggage arrivals hall that any conversation about Ryan's incredible revelation could commence.

'I just can't believe it,' whispered Doug, still utterly shell-shocked by what he had heard. 'Neither can I,' responded Ryan with a shake of his head. 'But the evidence I found couldn't have been any more conclusive. Like I said on the tape, my dad and his friends have been motivated by greed. It was all just a game to them. I didn't think they'd be capable of anything like this though, and I must admit I was tempted to turn a blind eye and just hope it all went away.'

Doug nodded in understanding, before affirming Ryan's decision to go to the police. 'You did the right thing. I can't imagine how difficult it must be to put your dad in the firing line like this, but maybe the punishment that follows will make him take a serious look at what he's done. Maybe it'll help him to understand there needs to be a change in his life.' Ryan stared at the floor as if lost in his thoughts, before replying, 'Cheers mate. I hope you're right.'

The baggage conveyer belt kicked into life with a dull thud, raising the volume in the arrival hall and allowing Doug and Ryan to speak a little more freely. 'Obviously what happens to my dad is my main concern, but I'm worried about what this could mean for the team as well,' said Ryan as the pair began to slowly make their way to the relevant conveyor belt. 'I wouldn't worry about that too much,' replied Doug. 'It'll be up to the police and the League Association to sort that out. Anyway, even if the other

Middlewood boys and I were at Bromfield for the wrong reasons, we were still playing for the right ones. I can safely say nobody in the dressing room was anything other than honest. We've been winning our games fair and square. Well, all of them apart from one by the sounds of it.'

Ryan cracked a brief smile for the first time in an hour or so, as if to acknowledge how implausible the entire situation was. 'Yeah, it's true. There's been honesty on the pitch even if there hasn't been too much off it. Hopefully that will count for something.'

Doug and Ryan waited a few minutes for their bags before heading out into the arrivals lounge. They were to be met by a driver who was going to take them to the city centre venue hosting the evening's awards ceremony. How strange, thought Doug, that just a few hours earlier there had been little else on his mind other than the prospect of having to face a media scrum asking him questions about passing his World Footballer of the Year award on to Luca Tavarno. Little did they know that in twenty-four hours they'd have far more pressing questions to ask about his season so far.

As expected, there were a couple of photographers and a television crew mixed in with the general public when Doug and Ryan stepped through the sliding doors out into the main body of the airport. They also spotted their driver among the assembly; a smartly dressed man holding a printed sign with the words 'Bromfield FC' emblazoned on it in large letters.

But before Doug could set off for his destination, there were to be a couple of quick words with the small press contingent. A microphone, camera and a couple of voice recorders were thrust in his face, with one Italian journalist doing the majority of the questioning in perfect English. 'Doug, welcome to Rome,' he began. 'Are you looking forward to the awards ceremony tonight? And how do you feel about handing your trophy over to the man that effectively forced you out of the limelight and into lower league football?'

'Wow, at least he gets straight to the point!' thought Doug as he composed himself for the cameras and offered his response. 'Well, Luca's a great player. It'll be an honour to hand him the award. Obviously my season panned out a little differently than I expected, but that's got more to do with my form than Luca's I think. I'm just looking forward to finishing the campaign with Bromfield and hopefully being back in the Premier League next season.'

Clearly looking for another angle on the story, the journalist probed a little further. 'It's looking like there could be two Italian teams in this season's Euro League final.

Do you think that proves, coupled with the fact an Italian player took your place at Middlewood, that Italian football is in a much healthier state than English football at the moment?'

Doug paused for a second before smiling at the interviewer and giving a tongue-in-cheek response. 'I'm not really sure about that,' he said, 'I'm Scottish'.

There were a couple of laughs and a couple more questions before the media's appetite was satisfied, and both Doug and Ryan shared a secret sense of relief that none of those questions related to off-field activities at Bromfield. That story obviously wasn't in the public domain – yet.

After the first of the day's press formalities were done with, Doug and Ryan headed towards their driver, who motioned to the front door of the airport and walked on ahead of them. Like many drivers who had picked Doug up on previous engagements around the globe, he had almost nothing to say for himself. A trait, thought Doug, more likely to relate to limited English skills and busy schedules than any lack of manners.

On arrival at the parked car, the driver unlocked the boot and loaded Doug and Ryan's bags into it before opening the doors for his passengers. As the two men took their seats in the luxurious vehicle, they were surprised to see another man occupying the front passenger seat. 'Oh, hello,' said Doug, 'Sorry if we kept you waiting.' The man, whose face was largely shielded by dark sunglasses, didn't turn around to respond. 'No problem,' came the reply, in a somewhat frosty tone. Doug and Ryan exchanged a glance, both of them clearly amused by the lack of a warm welcome they had been treated to by their designated drivers.

The car pulled off and left the airport behind, with Doug and Ryan now exchanging further small talk to keep their minds from the events likely to be unfolding back in the UK at that very moment. Soon though, they became aware that the car had left the motorway almost immediately after having gotten onto it. Ryan, a seasoned traveller, couldn't help but notice they had exited the lane marked for the city centre and were now passing through what looked like the industrial outskirts of Rome at a relatively slow pace. Loathed to question the judgement of their hosts, Ryan did his best to query their location politely. 'Is this a shortcut?' he said in his clearest Yorkshire accent. 'It's just that we don't have that long until we have to get to the awards.' There were a few seconds of silence from the front of the car, before the man in the passenger's seat again gave a two word reply. 'Yes, shortcut.'

Ryan leaned back into his seat, willing to accept the better navigational judgement of what he assumed were natives of the Italian capital. Before too much longer though, that judgement was becoming almost impossible to trust.

The car took another turn off what seemed to be a main road, passing through a quiet residential area lined with shabby looking apartments. And when the vehicle made yet another turn into a narrow lane with no pavements on either side, Ryan could no longer hold his protest. 'Look, I'm really sorry, but are we lost? We have to be at the awards ceremony soon and I was hoping we'd have some free time beforehand.' Despite the change in his tone, neither man appeared to be listening. And if they were, they certainly weren't responding. 'Excuse me,' said Ryan, attempting again to get an answer. This time it came.

As the car took one last turn into a secluded alley, the man in the passenger's seat turned around. In a thick London accent he replied. 'Will you shut up, son? We'll get where we're going soon enough. We just need to have a little chat first, all right?' Stunned and suddenly terrified, both Doug and Ryan slowly shifted their eyes from the gnarled face of their aggressor to the gun he was brandishing in their general direction.

Instinctively, both men burst into action and grabbed for their respective door handles in an effort to break free from the car. But their efforts were in vain, with both of the rear doors firmly locked. To make matters worse, their desperate actions inflamed the anger of the two men in the front of the car – the driver now drawing a weapon of his own and pointing it squarely in Ryan's face. 'All right, lads!' he spat in a furious and raised voice, 'Nobody's going anywhere! The child locks are on, but that doesn't mean we can't behave like grown-ups. Just sit tight, do as you're told and we'll get back on the road. Understand?'

Shaken, but realising they were completely trapped, Doug and Ryan gave a nod of acknowledgement and eased back into their seats – their eyes firmly fixed on the firearms being held just a matter of inches away from them.

'Right,' said the driver in a more controlled tone, 'That's better.' Casting a quick glance up and down the alley to ensure no passers-by were in the vicinity, he continued. 'We don't have very long, boys, so let's make this as quick as we can. Young Eaves, you've been a bit of a stupid boy, haven't you?'

Ryan, whose face was now completely white with shock, looked at Doug then back at the driver before mumbling a response. 'I, I don't know what you mean.'

The driver shook his head angrily, but his voice remained composed. 'Oh, I think you have been stupid. In fact, I know you have! I know you've been snooping around up at the stadium, reading things that weren't for you to read. Does that sound about right?'

This time, Ryan couldn't find any words of reply, and just stared blankly at the two men as the panic that had gripped him slowly gave way to confusion.

'I'll take your silence to mean you know exactly what I'm talking about,' snarled the driver. 'The thing is, young Eaves, you've made what we like to call a "schoolboy error". Isn't that right, Mick?' The man in the passenger's seat, who had now removed his sunglasses and held Doug in a steely gaze, cracked a wry smile. 'Oh yes, a definite schoolboy error,' he replied, his mocking voice designed to remind Doug and Ryan exactly who was in control.

The driver gave a brief laugh before elaborating. 'You see, rich kid, your schoolboy error was that after all your hard work reading and printing documents you shouldn't have, you put them in a big brown envelope and...' the driver paused for a second, smiled at Ryan, then said, 'Well, why don't you tell me what you did?'

Still visibly shaken, Ryan could see there was little point in denying the allegations. 'I sent it all to the police.' Almost before Ryan could finish his sentence, the driver started up again. 'Ah, but you didn't, did you? After all your hard work, you rounded up all those things you shouldn't have read, put them in a big brown envelope then – and I find this bit hard to take in – you left them in the office mail pile for someone to post in the morning! Seriously, son, that's one of the stupidest things I've ever heard!'

Ryan hung his head, apparently shamed into silence by the humiliating revelations and sarcastic laughter of the two men in the front of the car. If the documents had never made it to the police, then Ryan and Doug were the only people that knew the full extent of the illegal goings-on at Bromfield. And judging by the fact they now found themselves in the backstreets of a foreign city with guns pointed directly at them, there were people willing to go to any lengths to ensure their secret never saw the light of day.

Confirming these suspicions, the driver turned his attention to Doug. 'Can you believe that, Mackay?' he laughed, 'Sherlock Holmes here did all the hard work then left the evidence in plain sight of the wrong people. With friends like that, who needs enemies, eh?'

Realising that whatever he said to the two men would have no effect on the ultimate outcome of their predicament, Doug instead offered a word of encouragement to Ryan. 'Don't worry about it mate, everything will be fine,' he said.

As reassuring as the words were for Ryan, the driver didn't take kindly to them. For him, Doug's apparent calmness indicated he wasn't taking his captivity as seriously as he should be. In a sudden tirade, the short-tempered kidnapper launched into a sobering explanation of what the evening ahead held in store. 'I can promise you one thing, Mackay; things aren't going to be fine!' he snapped. 'Mixing with this young man was the biggest mistake you ever made, and I'll tell you why. In a matter of hours you'll be on the stage at the awards ceremony giving your precious trophy to a more deserving player. But here are the most important details you need to know: When you go inside, I'll go with you. The security men on the door will know my name, because we work for the same people. Everywhere you go, someone will be watching you. I'll be holding your hand backstage, and Eaves Jr. will keep his seat out here in the car with Mick. Isn't that right, Mick?' Mick nodded in feverish agreement but stayed silent so the driver could continue.

'If you try to talk to anyone, hand over a note, make a signal or run away, Mick will be one phone call away and your less-than-brilliant chum here will disappear without a trace. Even better than that though, Mackay – and I think you're going to like this – for the only few seconds I can't be beside you as you hand over your award on stage, you're going to be firmly in our sights.'

Doug, who, internally at least, was anything but the composed figure the driver had mistaken him for, shot a confused look in the direction of his captor.

'Don't look so puzzled, son,' came the response, 'It's really quite straightforward. Up in the gallery, out of sight to the average party guest, will be a friend of ours who really is a crack shot with a rifle. Any funny business on stage and you'll be making your exit in the most spectacular fashion you can imagine! And I'd be extra careful too; these snipers tend to get an itchy trigger finger on special occasions like this!'

The car fell silent for a moment as the full weight of what was unfolding hit Doug and Ryan. They were utterly ensnared, their knowledge of what was taking place at Bromfield shared only by the very people who would stop at nothing to prevent it being revealed. They had no choice but to play along; doing as they were instructed in constant awareness that one wrong move could be their last. But what would happen after the awards ceremony? How far would these men and the people they worked for go to ensure Doug and Ryan stayed silent? As the sheer gravity of their predicament took hold, the car engine sparked into life and the vehicle started to roll along the shadowy alley once more.

Unable to quash the thoughts now rising in his mind, Ryan spoke before the talkative driver had another opportunity. 'What are you going to do with us after the ceremony?' he asked. 'People will be looking for us, and you can't just make one of the world's most famous football players disappear.'

Both the driver and his accomplice gave another spiteful laugh. 'Don't you worry about it, young Eaves,' replied the driver. 'We're *bona fide* magicians me and Mick – we can make anyone disappear!'

The black car rolled into one of the VIP parking bays at the awards ceremony venue and slowly came to a halt. Doug and Ryan had remained in total silence for the duration of the drive into the city centre, each of them secretly thinking of ways in which they might be able to make good their escape.

In truth though, there was no way out. This message had been regularly reiterated to them by the driver as they sped towards their destination, a message that was all the easier to believe as his accomplice continued to observe them like a hungry hawk and aim his firearm briefly at one before tilting it in the direction of the other. There was no way to gesture to passing cars or pedestrians under such circumstances, though the car's blacked out windows would have rendered that an impossibility anyway.

Before stepping out of the car, Doug was reminded of the 'plan' one last time. 'All right lads, this is it,' asserted the driver; noticeably more focused and muted than before. 'Mackay, you come with me, master Eaves stays here for a nice evening in with Mick. If either one of you tries anything you shouldn't, I promise you'll regret it. After the ceremony, we come back to the car and set off on the final part of this little mystery tour. Should be quite a night, shouldn't it, Mick?'

As always, the sombre looking Mick was right on cue. 'A night to remember I'd say. A night to remember.'

With that, Doug was instructed to get out of the car, and before he could offer a final word of hope to Ryan, the chairman's son did the honours. 'Stay calm in there, Doug, you were right, everything will be fine.' The driver, who had already opened the car door and started to make his way out, couldn't resist having the final word. 'No, like I said boys, it won't be fine. Now shut up and let's go.'

Doug's door was unlocked and he stepped out into the balmy evening air. The small crowd of people making their way into the venue offered him a sudden rush of hope that there might be some way to secretly communicate his situation, but the presence of the driver at his side and the knowledge of Ryan locked securely in the car at the back of his mind quickly crushed any thoughts of such action. As they made their way through the main entrance, the driver made good on his promise to prove to Doug that he and Mick were not acting alone. 'Evening, Marco', he said as they breezed past the stocky security man on the door. 'Good evening, Mr Carlisle,' replied the bouncer, offering Doug a quick wink to acknowledge he was indeed in on the plan.

In the foyer, Doug began to bump into some familiar faces – with managers, fellow professionals and journalists grabbing the last of the complimentary food and drinks, but he found himself capable of nothing more than the most basic small talk before being greeted by one of the event organisers.

'Ah, hello Mr. Mackay,' said the friendly representative of the World Football Organisation. 'You're a little late, it might be best if you just come backstage with me. We're going to have the award handover in about 15 minutes.' Doug looked at the driver quickly, who continued to shadow him at a distance of no more than a yard or two. 'No problem,' replied Doug, 'Just lead the way.' The man from the WFO motioned and began to walk ahead, stopping in his tracks when he noticed that what looked like Doug's chauffeur was coming along too. 'Em, sorry sir, I can have someone show you to your seat if you like – we only need

Mr Mackay.' The driver gave a pleasant laugh and patted the man on the shoulder. 'Oh, no,' he said 'Mr Mackay insists I go everywhere with him. A little strange, I know, but he gets a bit lost in foreign countries! I'll just wait with him backstage.' The man from the WFO smiled and looked at Doug, who had no choice but to go along with the scam. They walked together to a door leading to the backstage area, providing a brief moment of respite which Doug used to say a silent prayer. 'Heavenly Father, I can't see any way out of this. I thank you that you are bigger than circumstances, and where we see no solution you can find one. I'm scared of what could happen to Ryan and me, and I just pray that you'll look after us and bring us safely through tonight.'

Moments later, Doug was in a darkened area next to the side of the stage. From where he was standing he could hear the accompanying music for a presentation that was currently taking place for the gathered media and public. A large screen was showing some of the finest moments from Luca Tavarno's season so far, with footage of his goals raining in against both domestic and international opposition. The man himself was backstage as well, accompanied by his agent, both of whom offered Doug a friendly wave upon his arrival and began to make their way over. Before they could reach him, the driver gave Doug one last reminder of his predicament. 'Mackay, take a quick look up to the back left corner of the auditorium. You see that black shape and tiny red right there? That's my friend I told you about – the one with the itchy trigger finger. One wrong move and you're a goner. You and your little chum in the car.'

The driver was telling the truth. Beyond rows of vacant seats in the second tier of the venue, Doug could make out the silhouette of a body lurking alone in the darkness. This operation to keep both him and Ryan silent apparently knew no bounds.

A moment later, Luca Tavarno was at Doug's side, offering his hand to his former Middlewood team-mate. Doug gladly returned the gesture, relieved beyond belief to see a familiar face in these most alien of circumstances. 'Hi Doug,' said Luca in his thick Italian English. 'Thanks for all the kind things you said in the newspapers about me. I appreciate it, and I'm sorry if all this is a bit awkward.'

In that moment it occurred to Doug he had the driver outnumbered. Luca was the closest thing he had to a friend in the auditorium. If he suddenly turned and launched at the driver, the Italian would surely join the attack. With the driver detained he could sneak back to the car ... The thought died as quickly as it had formed. Off in the shadows the knowledge of the sniper held him in invisible shackles. He couldn't take the risk, especially not with Ryan still at gunpoint. Snuffing out the thought, he replied to Luca. 'It's good to see you too. Everything I said about you in the papers was true; you've had a brilliant season. It's not awkward for me at all – you know how the press just likes to make a big deal of these things though.'

Luca nodded. 'Yes, definitely,' he replied, before adding, 'Hey, maybe next year we'll be playing up front for Middlewood together again. You've had a pretty amazing season yourself! And you never know what the future holds, right?'

Doug's opportunity to respond was snatched away by the driver, who seemed keen to remind him of his presence once more. With a broad grin he interrupted the exchange between the two football stars to offer his own insight. 'That's right, old friend – Doug has no idea what the future holds.'

All of a sudden, a deafening applause began to rise from the main body of the auditorium. The cheery man from the World Football Organisation buzzed back onto the scene and indicated to Doug and Luca that it was time to take the stage. Meeting the request, the two men stepped hastily towards the stairs at the side of the makeshift platform and made their way out into the combined glare of the spotlights and the world's sports media. Cameras flashed and the applause faded as they took their places either side of the WFO's president, Atholé Fournier. Both players were briefly introduced before Doug was handed the elaborate crystal trophy offered up on such occasions and asked to present it to Luca. Cradling the award in both hands, Doug stepped towards the mic and did his best to remain composed.

From where he was standing now, he had an even clearer view of the sniper positioned above and behind the unsuspecting assembly before him. From the corner of his eye, he was also able to catch an occasional glimpse of the driver, who had taken up a new position immediately at the foot of the stage stairs.

Doug cleared his throat. 'Good evening everyone,' he began, 'It's an honour to be here tonight and to hand this award to a player as talented as Luca Tavarno. I know a lot has been said about the fact our paths have crossed in a fairly unusual way this season, but as a football fan as well as a football player, I feel privileged to give this award to someone who represents attacking flair on the field, and is a true gentleman off it. Congratulations, Luca.'

And with that, Doug's duty was done. His kind words were met with more applause, but journalists in the front row typed frantically for the duration of his twenty second offering, reporting through their various media outlets that Doug was 'visibly shaken' and 'clearly upset' by the process of acknowledging his crown had passed on to another. How wrong they were.

If only they'd known that, as they watched him make his way off the stage, he was about to return into captivity. If only they'd known that his very departure from Middlewood had been a cynical money-making scheme by a criminal syndicate; that his misfortune stretched far beyond any events that had appeared in print that season.

He trudged wearily down the steps, exchanging a glance with the waiting driver as he did so. Had he missed his one chance to break free from his captors and reveal the truth behind Bromfield's season? Had he been a coward?

Following the driver's prompting, Doug began to walk with him back towards the car park. They would slip out before anyone could notice, although presumably the rumour mill would start back up with a vengeance when Doug didn't show face at the post-awards reception. As they left the venue and headed for the car, the driver spoke once more. 'Good boy. We didn't want to have to get rid of you in front of the cameras. Would have been a very messy business. Can't say I thought much of your speech though. Twenty seconds? I reckon I could have done better!'

Doug didn't respond. He had been taking events one step at a time since he and Ryan were captured earlier in the day, but what lay ahead was suddenly unknown. The threats that the driver and his accomplice had made over the last number of hours seemed real enough, and as soon as he was back in the car, any final hopes of escape would be crushed. Repeating his prayer from earlier in the evening, Doug took the final steps towards the car door and allowed himself to be bundled in by the driver.

But inside the vehicle, there was a surprise in store. Contrary to the planned chain of events, neither Ryan nor the indomitable Mick were present as expected. This fact had been hidden from Doug and the driver as they approached the car due to the blacked out windows, but the sheer horror that appeared to grip the driver upon opening his own door made it clear that this sudden disappearance was not part of the plan. Recoiling in shock, the baffled driver let out a yell. 'Mick?! Mick?! What's going on?!' Doug's pulse quickened, and he realised this was his chance. He leapt towards the door handle on the opposite side of the car and swung the door wide open. Springing into the car park, he fought the wave of sudden dizziness that had taken hold of him and prepared to sprint into the clear. But before he could even start to run, the driver's shouting was drowned out by an even louder cacophony. There was a thunderous clatter of feet charging towards the car, and what sounded like a dozen voices screaming all at once: 'Drop your weapon! Get down! Get down! You're under arrest!'

Doug fell to the ground, covering his head with his hands, but it was not him they had come for. From a convoy of parked vans around the corner, an assembly of policemen had pounced, sprinting headlong at the driver and tackling him to the ground with a crushing thud. Doug dared to look up, aware now that he had not been the target of the operation. As he did so, he was stunned to see Ryan quickly making his way towards him. Utterly speechless, Doug had to be hauled to his feet by his friend, who greeted him with an embrace and repeated those most reassuring of words, 'It's all right. Everything's all right.'

In a frantic blur of activity and action, the hopelessness of the moment had suddenly turned to sheer joy. Catching his breath, but still wide-eyed in utter wonder, Doug asked the obvious question. 'Ryan, what happened? How did you get away?'

Wearing the most tangible expression of relief Doug had ever seen, Ryan sighed and smiled, before explaining, 'There was another envelope of evidence, Doug – one that did make it to the police.'

As journalists, photographers and film crews began arriving on the scene to investigate the commotion that had so suddenly erupted, Doug shook his head and looked at Ryan. 'You know, it never ceases to amaze me,' he said.

Ryan raised his eyebrows, still wearing a broad grin. 'What never ceases to amaze you, mate?' he enquired.

'The way God answers our prayers,' replied Doug. 'It still blows my mind every time.'

A few hours later, after assisting the police in their investigations and getting a routine once-over at the hospital, Doug and Ryan found themselves on the roof of their plush Rome hotel.

With the details of the evening's events starting to grip the media in a mild fever, the hotel foyer was becoming increasingly populated with sports journalists pursuing the inside scoop on what had taken place. In no mood to talk or speculate over the breaking news they found themselves at the centre of, the pair had sought out the roof terrace for a quiet setting in which to dissect the day.

'So, you reckon there was actually a sniper in the auditorium? Or was it a bluff?'

queried Ryan, he and Doug both now cutting considerably more laid-back figures than they had amid the tension of the afternoon and evening.

'Oh, it wasn't a bluff! No way!' retorted Doug. 'I could see the guy up in the shadows. Seriously scary stuff, you'll be glad you were left in the car!'

Ryan chuckled. 'What, in the car with Mick? I wouldn't even wish that on you, mate, he was a serious villain!'

The buzz of the city streets hung in the night air as the two men fell silent for a moment. 'I always wanted to come to Rome,' uttered Ryan, standing to his feet to take in the dimly lit skyline a little more closely. 'Yeah,' said Doug, 'It's a nice place when you're not being kidnapped by Mick and Co. You should come back some day.'

Ryan looked at Doug and laughed again. 'You're joking now, mate, but that was seriously scary earlier on. I've got no idea how you kept your cool. I thought we were going to, you know...'

Doug nodded. 'Yeah, I know, things were looking bad. But I was anything but cool Ryan – I was terrified!'

Ryan fixed his stare on Doug and raised his eyebrows. 'Well, you had me fooled. You seemed pretty peaceful from where I was sitting!'

Doug joined Ryan on his feet and the two men ambled over to the edge of the roof terrace, leaning on a railing and watching as a moped driver in the street below sped the wrong way down a narrow one-way street.

Ryan broke the silence. 'That stuff you said earlier, about the power of prayer, you really believe in that, don't you?'

Doug nodded. 'I definitely do. I've seen so many situations that seemed like they had no solution being turned on their head, and I'm certain it's down to God.'

'You're certain? I wish I could be certain of something I can't see!' replied Ryan.

'I suppose that's the thing,' responded Doug. 'I feel like I can see evidence of His power everywhere. I've had a faith for a long time and I find it harder not to believe, if you know what I mean? Someone once described it to me as being a bit like the wind – you can't see it, but you can see its effects everywhere.'

Ryan stared off into the distance. 'I think I would have said I believed in God once, when I was younger. But everyone in church just seemed like hypocrites to me. They were all there praying on a Sunday and then the rest of the week ... well, they just didn't seem to act on what they said they believed. I figured if that's what Christianity is all about, I can live without it.'

Doug offered another nod of acknowledgement. 'I know what you mean. I had my doubts when I was younger as well. But eventually it clicked that we shouldn't look at other people to form our opinions about God; we should look at his Son, Jesus. The Bible says he was the only perfect person who ever lived.'

Ryan took a sip from the coffee cup he was holding, realising the contents had gone cold. 'I'll be honest, Doug, I wasn't really listening in Sunday School – only enough to know Jesus was supposed to have turned water into wine then risen from the dead. How that affects me is the part I could never figure out!'

Doug paused for a moment. 'You remember that free kick I scored against Southfield on my debut for Bromfield?' he asked.

'Oh yeah! That was a peach, mate! What's that got to do with Jesus though? You about to tell me it was a miracle goal or something?'

Doug laughed. 'No, no,' he replied. 'But if they put together a DVD of my best goals, I'd like that to be on there. But there are other moments on the pitch – and off it – that I'm not so proud of though.'

Ryan cast a quizzical glance at Doug, who reached for a leather-bound menu from one of the nearby tables and held it flat in his right hand. 'Imagine this is a DVD – a highlight reel of your life,' he said. Ryan tilted his head. 'All right,' he replied, 'But I've never scored a goal like that I'm afraid!'

'Not to worry,' chuckled Doug. 'Imagine it has all your greatest moments and achievements captured on it; your graduation, nice things you've done for people – Ryan Eaves' greatest hits, if you will!'

'Good stuff!' laughed Ryan, 'I'll need to get a few copies made!'

Doug nodded. 'Yeah, but now imagine it's got those moments you're not so proud of. Times you hurt people's feelings, things you did that you felt you shouldn't have – things you did that nobody ever saw and you would never, ever want them to.' Ryan's face straightened. 'You still want me to run off a few copies?' enquired Doug. 'Not really,' responded Ryan. 'I've done some pretty shameful stuff, mate, I think I'd settle for nobody seeing the good things if they're going to get to see the bad things as well.'

'Same here,' said Doug. 'I don't think anyone would ever want that DVD of their life to get out.'

There was another silence as Doug continued to balance the menu in his hand.

'No offence, Doug, but what's this got to do with, you know, Jesus?'

Doug held up his free hand to assure Ryan he was getting to the point. 'The Bible says

that none of us are really good people –
that all those things we do that we're utterly
ashamed of and we know we shouldn't do
are a result of something called sin. It says
that every single one of us – no matter how
many "good" highlights we have – is so far
short of God's perfect standard that we're
going to have to be punished for that sin.
According to the Bible, only one person has
ever lived a perfect life.'

Ryan gestured skyward. 'Jesus?' he
enquired. 'Right,' replied Doug.

Ryan smiled. 'I'm glad that was the right
answer; it's the one I always gave in Sunday
School as well!'

Doug returned his smirk. 'Ryan, I believe
that God loved sinners so much that he sent
Jesus into the world on a rescue mission.
He came to rescue us from the punishment
for sin, all that stuff on the highlights DVD
we're ashamed of. Without him, none of us
can ever have a relationship with God. But
because of his amazing, undeserved love for
sinful people, God chose to act...'

Doug placed his left hand on the menu
lying in his hand, then flipped his right hand
over so it was suddenly free. '... which means
all that garbage we do is transferred from
us to him. Jesus could have stayed put in
heaven, but instead he chose to come into
the world, hang on a cross and rise three
days later, so that we didn't need to stay

separated from God. He takes the blame for us, he pays the price we should and at the same time he gives us his perfect life so that we can be blameless before God and enjoy His presence forever. He's our substitute, and in life – unlike when I'm playing football – I believe I really need a substitute to take my place, because I'll never live up to God's standards. Nobody will. I said sorry to God for turning my back on him and put my trust in Jesus when I was a young man, and it's the best decision I ever made.'

Ryan fixed his eyes on Doug's free right hand, then switched his attention to the menu now weighing on his left hand.

'I've never really heard it explained like that Doug, I must admit,' said Ryan, now shifting his gaze back to the Rome skyline. 'It sounds like there's more to this Jesus bloke than I knew. Maybe I should have been listening in Sunday School after all.'

Doug smiled. 'Well,' he said, 'unlike us, God doesn't change over the years. The offer of a new life through Jesus still stands.'

Both men stood in the still of the night and gazed into the distance as the sound of car horns and muffled shouts continued to drift upwards and then evaporate into the humid air circulating the city. It had been a day neither of them would ever forget.

The Final Act

And so it was that the curtain came down on the extraordinary events that had taken place behind the scenes at Bromfield and Middlewood that season.

Despite the cruel allegations of the two men that had held Doug and Ryan hostage in Rome, Ryan had not been as foolish as they hoped. For while he had indeed been ruled by old habits in placing one envelope of evidence in the stadium's standard outgoing mail pile, the other had arrived at a safer destination.

Aware that Ally had himself been a victim of the shady events, he knew he could trust Doug's closest friend and agent with the information that laid out the full extent of what had transpired over the course of the year.

On the day Doug and Ryan travelled to Rome, Ally awoke to find the envelope of incriminating facts resting behind his front door and immediately set out for the local police station to share the unthinkable details contained within.

As Doug and Ryan sat at gunpoint in a darkened street just outside Rome, an operation had already been set in motion on home soil to arrest the chief perpetrators in the scandal. Eddie Craven and three of his fellow board members at Middlewood were the first to receive knocks at the door from the police, with Ryan's father, David Eaves, next in line.

There was a tangled mess to unravel for the authorities. Who had the initial idea to turn Bromfield into a side capable of winning the First Division then bet tens of thousands of pounds on them actually doing so? Were all five men behind the plot equally responsible for the kidnapping of Doug and Ally on the night they played Lancaster? And who had directed the horrible events in Rome when it came to light that the entire scandal was on the verge of being uncovered?

In investigations by both the police and League Association, it was clear that all five men at the centre of the plot had enjoyed varying levels of involvement. The chief perpetrator was Middlewood's chief executive, Eddie Craven. He admitted to hatching the plan with David Eaves during a round of golf; saying it had all started out as nothing more than an amusing diversion before turning sour. Wary that the scam would be uncovered, Craven organised to have all the players loaned from Middlewood to Bromfield and their closest representatives watched closely from the moment they left for their new club.

His investment appeared to have paid off when reports got back to him that Doug's agent was getting close to the truth about the illegal payment made to Mileno at the outset of the affair. It was then that he and his three fellow directors at Middlewood used some old criminal connections to have Ally and Doug kidnapped and threatened. When the police seemed to be unable to find any evidence that would unravel the kidnapping, Craven and co. decided the best option was to refrain from any other such acts of intimidation.

But they were still concerned with their investment on the pitch. Some of the data Ryan recovered showed that all five men, including his father, had been involved in paying off the referee prior to Bromfield's crunch game with Wexvale. As Ryan suspected, they were determined to get three points from their toughest game of the season at all costs.

For his part, David Eaves had become increasingly consumed by the fear of being caught for his actions, and was responsible for calling his co-conspirators at Middlewood on the day he found the envelope of evidence at Old Mayfield. Unaware the incriminating details had been compiled by his son, or that his call to Eddie Craven would result in the kidnapping of Doug and Ryan in Rome, he urged Craven to do 'whatever was necessary' to ensure the truth didn't come out.

It was only when Ally drew the police's attention to the source of the evidence and informed them where Doug and Ryan were going to be that evening that alarm bells were raised and an international operation was set in motion to ensure the safety of the two men in Rome. When he realised that his involvement had endangered the life of his own son, David Eaves had broken down in tears, apologising for the near disastrous consequences of his role. 'It was all meant to be a joke,' he said, repeating the line in what was more heartfelt remorse than a vain final effort to be absolved of his crimes. It was no small comfort, then, when he was first reunited with Ryan and discovered that his son was not only unharmed, but willing to forgive him for the shameful events that had taken place.

In the two weeks that had now passed since Doug and Ryan's ordeal in Rome, many decisions had been made.

A judge ruled that Eddie Craven, David Eaves and the three others involved should all spend time behind bars to reflect on their actions, while the League Association banned them for life from any future involvement with clubs in England; a ban the World Football Organisation was happy to impose on a global basis. There would also be hefty financial penalties to pay. After all, if money was so precious to these men the press had now dubbed the 'Fixing Five', taking it away seemed like a fitting aspect of their punishment. There was also to be financial penalties for Mileno for their acceptance to walk away from their attempts to secure Doug after being paid off, while the referee in charge for the farcical Wexvale game paid with his career.

The fallout of the scandal didn't end there though. With clear evidence to show Bromfield's game against Wexvale had been fixed, the club would have to pay a collective price. Three points were subtracted from their overall tally for the season, causing them to drop from fourth to sixth in the league. That in itself offered cause for controversy.

Finishing sixth meant Bromfield had clinched the final place available in the First Division play-offs – affording them an opportunity to win promotion to the Premier League. Already devoting a majority share of their coverage to the scandal, the country's football media was awash every day with criticism from fans, managers and chairmen at rival clubs claiming Bromfield had no right to challenge for the most lucrative prize in world football. Promotion to the Premier League meant a cash injection for the lucky club of no less than sixty million pounds. How, asked critics, could Bromfield possibly be allowed to compete for such a grand sum after effectively cheating their way to victory during the course of the season?

But the League Association – not to mention many fair-minded football fans – saw it differently. Doug and his team-mates from Middlewood were victims as well. And while the reason for their being at Bromfield had sinister undertones, there was nothing illegal about the paperwork that had taken them from the heart of London to the humble surroundings of Old Mayfield.

In a statement to the press and public, League Association director Martin Ferguson made it clear that he felt Bromfield Football Club had suffered enough. The statement read: 'While we at the League Association recognise the extremely serious nature of the events at Bromfield FC this season, we are in agreement that the punishments handed out are appropriate in light of the fact that no player at the club has shown anything other than utmost integrity over the course of the season. Evidence proves there was only one game in which Bromfield was given an unfair advantage by corrupt officiating, and three points have been deducted accordingly. We are in overwhelming agreement that the chief victims of these scandalous events have been the Bromfield fans and players, who will live forever with a dark cloud over their reputations because of the actions of a handful of corrupt individuals.'

Whatever anyone else thought or said, that was the final word on the matter.

Doug pulled his laces tight and closed his eyes. In a matter of minutes he'd be taking the field for one of the biggest games of his life.

He pictured the scene that awaited him – the arena, the perfect pitch, the supporters. He imagined the sights and sounds, silently preparing himself for the exhilarating roar that would inevitably engulf the national stadium when the teams took the field.

A week earlier he had done the same as he readied himself for the second leg of Bromfield's play-off semi-final. With the time for talking about the controversies of the season behind them, Bromfield's players had lined up against third placed Avon United in a bid to take the penultimate step in their quest to reach the Premier League. The first leg of the tie had taken place at Avon's ground, Elmbank Road, and it couldn't have gone better for Bromfield. Fired up by the criticism levelled at the club from a number of detractors, Bromfield's players set a fierce pace from the outset; racing into a 2-0 lead before half-time with goals from Doug and Rob Barkly, who had now been accommodated in Clive Carswell's system to play up front alongside Doug after striking up a strong rapport with him on and off the pitch. In the second half, a dazzling solo effort from Hicham Morocci rounded off the scoring, placing Bromfield in the strongest position imaginable before the return match at Old Mayfield.

Their position was so strong, in fact, that Clive Carswell saw fit to leave Doug and fellow loan player Keith Davis on the bench in order to rest them for the likely play-off final just around the corner. Not only did the decision pay off, with Carswell's team running out 1-0 winners, it also served to show that even against the top teams in the league, Bromfield had more to offer than just the magic of Doug Mackay.

If the young team had started out as little more than a joke to two men playing a round of golf, they had grown into something entirely different since the turn of the year. Learning from the experience of their incoming Middlewood team-mates, Bromfield's less fashionable squad members had been forged into a battling force under the intense glare of the media, the criticism of rival fans and the desire to prove there was more to Bromfield FC than the star players they had become best known for. This team had come a long way from the shambolic scenes that took place in their first training session with Doug and his Middlewood colleagues, and were now ready to fight all for one and one for all to ensure their names were written forever in the club's history books. And it was a good job too, because the challenge that awaited them in the play-off final would demand nothing less than the sheer grit and determination of men willing to lay everything on the line.

As if the script for Bromfield's season so far hadn't been far-fetched enough, the final act ensured the intensity would remain in place right up until the closing minute, with the opposition for their final encounter guaranteed to carry no less motivation or righteous anger into the battle.

Wexvale Rovers had emulated Bromfield's passage into the play-off final with an equally impressive aggregate victory. Back in top form after a temporary dip that saw them fall out of the two automatic promotion spots in the First Division, Wexvale had battered local rivals Southfield 5-1 over the course of their semi-final matches.

It was no secret that a potential showdown between Wexvale and Bromfield was on the cards, and the battling club from the south had no intention of letting the opportunity slip through their fingers.

In the aftermath of being cheated out of three points by the underhanded events at Bromfield, Wexvale had hit a bad patch – submitting a healthy lead in the league table as their burning sense of indignation seemed to follow them onto the pitch. For the club's fans, Bromfield represented the primary reason they weren't in the Premier League already, and there was no way they were about to let their northern rivals snatch their place away from them again. Never mind the facts of the matter, when the people of Wexvale thought of Bromfield, they simply thought 'cheats'.

'We're not really thinking about the sixty million pounds,' said outspoken Wexvale manager Cliff Hayles in his final press conference before the match, 'this is about justice.'

Opening his eyes again, Doug turned to face the centre of the dressing room, where Bromfield manager Clive Carswell was preparing to offer his final words of motivation. 'Listen up!' he started, 'This is it, lads. We're all sick of what's surrounded us at the club this season, but the fact is, we've reacted like real men in the midst of it all. The criticism, the controversy – it's made us stronger, and pulled us together. And I'm proud of you for that.' He paused for a moment and looked around the room at his players.

'This has been the most incredible season most of us will ever experience, but this story isn't finished yet. Now's our chance to put a full stop after everything that's been said, and show everyone what Bromfield is really all about.'

His sentiments were met with raucous applause and shouts of encouragement from the team, who were at full strength and raring to go. The manager was right; there was no better way to silence the critics than to win the play-off final and take their place among football's elite in the Premier League.

Making their way into the tunnel, players from both sides lined up alongside each other in preparation for their march onto the hallowed turf of the national stadium. No words or glances were exchanged between the opposing sides; their minds collectively drifting to the thought that 90,000 fans about to explode in anticipation lay just a short walk away. It was a dizzying prospect, and a mixture of nerves and excitement took hold of each and every player as the referee began to lead the would-be heroes onto the pitch. Even Doug, who had stepped into action on the biggest sporting stages of all, was gripped by the tangible sense of occasion. As was the case with most of the players taking part that day, his parents and closest friends and family would be among the number inside the ground – a sure-fire way to ensure he was even more keyed up for action than usual.

Then came the roar; an eruption of noise from the stands as the twenty-two men about to do battle on behalf of their club's faithful fans stepped out into the blinding summer sunlight. Engulfing one half of the arena, forty-five thousand Wexvale fans brandished black and gold flags as they chanted their team's name over and over with every ounce of their energy. Equally full, and equally loud, the Bromfield end appeared as a sea of red and white from a distance, the tens of thousands of fans crammed in there unable to even hear the noise of the chanting Wexvale fans over their own deafening cries of 'Bromfield! Bromfield! Bromfield!'

As the national anthem played, the television cameras panned along the line-up of players. There was an impressive amount of talent on the field. Despite having been relegated from the Premier League the previous season, Wexvale Rovers had managed to retain many of their top players. In a day when loyalty and football were becoming increasingly less familiar bedfellows, Wexvale's stars had pledged to stay put and give their all in a bid to get the club back where they felt they belonged. There was Daryl Thomas, the six foot four inch former England international, who had made a habit of scoring vital goals for his country in years gone by and still had plenty to offer at club level. Out wide on the right was Kyle Robertson, whose blend of pace and precision crossing had played no small part in his team-mate Thomas notching up the 23 goals that had made him the most prolific striker in the league. And then there was Phil Hughes; the young forward who had been unjustly dismissed from the action on the day Bromfield had been given more than a little help from the corrupt referee. The memory of sitting in the dressing room that day after first being accused of diving and then sent off for his indignant reaction was still very fresh in his mind. Like every player in a Wexvale jersey, he was ready for revenge.

Next, the camera worked its way along the Bromfield line-up. If fans of the now-famous club were worried by the rich offering of talent on display for Wexvale, they were surely breathing a little easier after a look at what they brought to the table.

Yuri Dvorchek, Keith Davis and Hicham Morocci were all fully fit and ready to play, providing sheer star quality at the back, in the middle and out wide for Bromfield. Each of the former Middlewood players' names was cheered to the rafters as they were announced over the stadium's speaker system, but the loudest roar of all was reserved for number 24, Doug Mackay. Not only had his raft of goals provided points and dazzling entertainment in equal measure, his cool head and apparent determination to bring the team together in their unusual circumstances had endeared him forever to the Bromfield faithful. As far as they were concerned, if it wasn't for Doug, they wouldn't have been at the stadium at all that day.

With the remainder of their team, especially Rob Barkly, also now playing at a level most would have considered impossible a matter of months ago, there were numerous reasons to be optimistic.

With the pomp and ceremony now concluded, the teams took up their positions either side of the halfway line and waited for the referee to signal the kick off. As had been the case all afternoon, the national stadium was a cauldron of noise, colour and anticipation.

Wexvale got things underway, knocking the ball back deep into their own half before attempting to play a long pass forward to Daryl Thomas. Keith Davis rose with Thomas to meet the incoming ball, clattering hard into the big striker in the process. It was a foul, but nothing too cynical. For the Wexvale fans, however, it was their cue to strike up a chant that would echo around the stadium for much of the afternoon. 'Cheats! Cheats! Cheats!' they screamed, reminding

Bromfield's fans and the huge audience watching on TV that they had definitely not forgotten what happened when the two teams last locked horns.

The resulting free kick was whipped into the box by Kyle Robertson, but was safely claimed by Bromfield goalie Tommy Bjarnason. It proved to be a familiar scene for much of the first half.

As was so often the case in the most vital games of all, the two teams were so determined not to concede a goal that they stuck like glue to their opposite numbers, cancelling out the efforts of one another and making for a game that was much higher on tension than entertainment.

Time and again, defenders threw long balls forward just above or beyond their waiting strikers and into the clutches of the opposing goalkeeper, and a series of niggling fouls ensured free-flowing football was kept to a minimum. To cap the frustrations of the tightly marked Bromfield players, the deafening chorus of boos that struck up every time one of them touched the ball was a demoralising reminder that in this particular pantomime, they were the arch-villains.

Unsurprisingly, the breakthrough came when the frustrating trend in play ceased momentarily. Breaking quickly after a Bromfield corner, Wexvale fullback Rodrigo Lima found some space to run into before spaying a cross-field pass to Kyle Robertson. The speedy winger took the ball in his stride and drove deep into the right-hand channel of the field. From there he waited for support, which was forthcoming in the form of Phil Hughes. A quick one-two with Hughes saw Robertson receive the ball once more, only now he was on the edge of the Bromfield box. Cutting outside the last defender in his path, Robertson took a speculative effort on goal. It wasn't his best strike of the season, but it carried with it an element of surprise that left Tommy Bjarnason at full stretch in a desperate effort to tip the ball behind the goal. Unfortunately for him, not to mention the forty-three thousand Bromfield fans in attendance, he only succeeded in tipping it straight into the path of Phil Hughes; who had continued his run in the hope of a return pass from his team-mate. Presented with a gaping goal, Hughes did what he was best at and pummelled the ball into the back of the net to put his side ahead.

Coming only two minutes before half-time, the breakaway goal was a sickening blow for Bromfield, but clearly the sweetest tonic everyone connected to Wexvale Rovers could ever have asked for. Their supporters, players and coaching staff danced and punched the air with vigorous abandon. Clearly they'd been waiting for this moment for a long time, and they had every intention of revelling in it.

Minutes later, the referee blew his whistle to signal half-time, and the Bromfield players trudged off with a feeling of frustration weighing heavy on their shoulders. Their fans were silent; painfully aware that Wexvale's tight marking, hard tackling and one goal advantage were going to be hard to overcome. Was this most promising of days destined to end in abject disappointment? It was certainly starting to look that way.

The first to arrive back in the dressing room was Doug, who slumped onto a bench and took a sip of an energy drink. He could feel the frustration of his team-mates as they followed him in one after another; their heads hanging low and their hopes of a glorious victory slowly unravelling.

In the moments before Clive Carswell arrived to offer his take on the first half, Doug cast his mind back over the turbulent season so far. He remembered the excitement he had felt on his Middlewood debut, the terror he had endured as he and Ally fled their captors at the warehouse, and the sheer joy of an answered prayer as the hopelessness he had felt in Rome gave way to unbridled relief. But most of all he remembered the afternoon he had spent in his apartment reading the Bible and praying for peace in the midst of his shaky start to life in the Premier League. The words he had read that day returned with crystal clarity: 'For surely I know the plans I have for you, says the Lord, plans for your welfare and not for harm, to give you a future with hope.'

How true that was. For all the bleak moments he had endured, Doug's future was full of hope. He had been kept safe in nightmarish circumstances, given the opportunity to show God's love in an unexpected environment and remained certain that whatever lay around the corner, his Creator would always be in total control.

Just as had been the case on that snowy afternoon in December, Doug felt peace take hold of him; a sense of freedom that could only come from a higher power.

At that moment, Clive Carswell addressed his weary charges for the last time that season. 'All right boys, just relax,' he said. 'I know it's been frustrating, but we're only halfway there. There's still time. All we're lacking is a little spark of imagination. Just let your football do the talking; try things you'd only usually try on the training ground. Take players on, shoot from anywhere and everywhere and show these hatchet men that the beautiful game always beats the ugly one.'

Following some fine-tuning of tactics and motivational words from experienced squad members like Doug and Keith Davis, it was time for the restart.

With the renewed optimism that magically awakens in football fans during the half-time break, the Bromfield faithful were back in full voice – believing again that their side could yet turn the tide. The Wexvale fans were buoyant too, continuing their singing and chanting of songs that both paid homage to their own team and disparaged their opponents.

From the outset of the second half, it was clear the next forty-five minutes would be more exciting than the last. Two minutes after the restart, Hicham Morocci finally showed some of his trademark skill and found an inch or two of space with a deft touch that left a Wexvale defender trailing in his wake. His fine footwork was matched by an equally eye-catching cross that found Rob Barkly just inside the eighteen yard box. Taking one touch, Rob struck an effort goal-ward, forcing a fine save from Wexvale's number one, Shane Quinn. As disappointing as it was to see the ball firmly in the opposing keeper's clutches once more, it was a sign of life that prompted a thunderous cheer to spread through the ranks of action-starved Bromfield fans. It was also a sign of what was to come.

Bromfield's big-name players had come out firing on all cylinders, with Yuri Dvorchek now dominating the midfield, Keith Davis bossing the Wexvale strikers at the back and Hicham Morocci finding more and more space to launch crosses into the box. Doug too was finding room to play, although he still remained under closer guard than any other Bromfield player on the pitch. It was a compliment of sorts, if an unappealing way to spend your afternoon.

Sooner or later, something had to give. The Bromfield fans were still on their feet following their last attack when Dvorchek dispossessed his opposite number in the centre of the field. Without looking up, he instinctively picked out Morocci with a curling pass out wide. As he was now doing with alarming regularity, Morocci ghosted past his marker and headed towards the byline. This time, his cross was deeper than he had intended, flying to the opposite corner of the field. But just when it looked like the ball was about to roll out of play, Doug shook off his marker and prevented it from doing so. With his back to goal, and a Wexvale central defender bearing down on him, Doug remembered Clive Carswell's words: 'Try things you'd only usually try on the training ground.'

'Well,' thought Doug, 'It's worth a shot.' Aware that the incoming defender was now only a yard or two behind, Doug rolled the ball out to the side with his right foot, hoping the defender behind him would mirror his action. Indeed he did, and with a neat flick of his foot, Doug knocked the ball backwards through his own legs, and the legs of the baffled Wexvale player. It was a sublime piece of skill, but Doug wasn't finished yet.

Now in line with the six yard box but still at the far side of the pitch, Doug jinked towards the corner of the 18 yarder, well aware that two more Wexvale defenders were making a beeline straight for him – this time from the front. Looking up, and with only a split second to spare before the moment was gone, Doug struck the ball with the inside of his foot, sending a spinning, curling shot in the direction of the goal. At first it looked like it was destined to end up high and wide, but Doug wasn't World Footballer of the Year for nothing. At the last instant, the perfectly hit ball dipped and bent inches over the outstretched hand of Wexvale's sprawling keeper and flew straight into the opposite top corner of the net. If Doug's skill in the corner was special, the finish was out of this world.

Finally the Bromfield fans and players could celebrate. It had taken seventy-six minutes for the goal to come, and the ecstatic reaction of everyone in red and white spoke of their sheer relief at being back in the game. Doug was mobbed by team-mates as he wheeled away from the spot where he'd struck the ball, and quickly found himself at the bottom of the highest pile-up the national stadium had ever witnessed. Now the Bromfield fans truly believed again; with fourteen minutes still to go, maybe they could even snatch a precious winner before ever having to contemplate the looming prospect of extra time and penalties.

To Wexvale's credit though, they weren't about to lie down and admit defeat. They had been outplayed in the second half, but the game wasn't finished yet. And with the likelihood that the next goal would now decide the final outcome, their frustrated players mustered the will for one last effort – shouting words of encouragement at one another and urging the closest player in black and gold to rediscover their fighting spirit.

Suddenly both teams were playing with total abandon, leaving gaps at the back, surging forward at every opportunity and expending every last ounce of energy left in their weary legs.

With six minutes to play, Wexvale's familiar long ball tactics suddenly returned an opening. Picking up a pass launched over the heads of the Bromfield back four, Daryl Thomas charged into the box and found himself one-on-one with Tommy Bjarnason. With the television commentators howling with excitement and the Wexvale fans ready to erupt in celebration, Thomas chipped the ball over the stranded keeper, only to see it strike the underside of the bar and bounce down inches in front of the goal line. Sprinting to pick up the loose ball, a melee of players scrambled across the box to claim a decisive touch. Daryl Thomas and Keith Davis arrived at the same moment, sliding in unison towards the now stationary football. It was Thomas who got there first though, prodding the ball goal-ward and lying where he landed to watch it cross the line. But it never did.

Keith Davis may have arrived a second later than his former England team-mate Thomas, but he still managed to secure a second touch on the ball, forcing it inches to the side and back into the arms of the now-recovered Tommy Bjarnason. It was the closest call imaginable, and the most agonising moment conceivable for the Wexvale support.

In the heat of the moment, Davis and Thomas had both got a piece of each other as well as the ball, and both of them sprung to their feet abruptly to accuse the other of sticking the boot in. In scenes reminiscent of the battle at Wexvale's Carlston stadium earlier in the season, players now waded in recklessly and started a mass shoving-match that reignited the bad blood which had simmered for so long between the clubs.

This time there were no red cards to be seen when the messy affair was over, just bookings for chief perpetrators Daryl Thomas and Keith Davis. The spat also served to ensure the ninety thousand supporters cranked the atmosphere up to a new level of intensity as the game entered its final few minutes.

Waiting upfield for Tommy Bjarnason to take a goal kick which had just been awarded following the breakdown of Wexvale's latest attack, Doug was longing for one more opening to come his way. He still felt relatively fresh, but knew that Wexvale's renewed vigour made extra time a dangerous proposition.

As if his team-mate had heard his silent hopes, Doug saw the ball heading straight for him as he waited just over the halfway line. Jostling with his marker for some precious space, Doug got to the incoming ball first and knocked it out wide with one touch to the ever-ready Morocci.

Twisting back inside and darting down the centre of the field, Doug started a run towards the far side of the box in anticipation of a possible Morocci cross. The little winger still had a lot to do though, and when Wexvale fullback Rodrigo Lima successfully dispossessed him and kicked the ball into touch for a throw-in, the rest of the Wexvale defence reassembled and ensured Doug and Rob Barkly were as tightly marked as was allowed within the rules of the game.

There were now ninety minutes on the clock, and with only a couple likely to be added for the earlier altercation, extra time now seemed like the most likely outcome.

The throw in by Morocci was picked up and worked infield to Dvorchek, who spread the play out wide again to Bromfield winger, Leighton Cook. Cook, the youngest player on the Bromfield side, drove into the space left open to him by the retreating Wexvale backline. Sensing this could be his team's final opportunity, Doug surged out of the box to make himself available for a pass. Cook duly obliged, knocking the ball into Doug's feet and bringing the Bromfield fans to theirs once more. There was still work to be done though, and with a wall of black and gold shirts blocking Doug's path into the opposition box, he opted to pass as well – finding Rob open inside, but also limited by the tangle of defenders before him.

There was always a way to make space though, and the instant Doug side-footed the ball to Rob, he set off on another run designed to breach the ragged Wexvale backline. Banking on Doug's actions, Rob quickly chipped the ball into the Wexvale box, timing it to perfection to ensure his team-mate was onside and through on goal. Gratefully accepting the precision pass, Doug found himself in the clear just 16 yards out. A tidal wave of noise spread through every inch of the stadium as the star striker composed himself and prepared to hammer home the decisive blow.

But it wasn't to be. At the very instant his right boot was about to connect with the ball, Doug was sent tumbling to the ground by a desperate lunge from behind. In the heat of battle, Wexvale captain Billy Clark had lost his head and performed the most blatant of fouls at the worst possible instant.

There was only one conceivable outcome, and every single one of the ninety thousand attendees in the national stadium knew it: penalty.

No protests were forthcoming from the Wexvale players as they resigned themselves to the grim reality now unfolding. One or two sprinted towards the goalkeeper to offer a spirited pep-talk before the kick was taken, while thousands of Wexvale fans clasped their hands above their heads in disbelief. Behind the goal where the spot-kick was to be taken, Bromfield's loyal followers danced in jubilation and embraced one another as a surge of nervous energy swept through their ranks and united them in unbearable anticipation.

No questions were asked in the stands when Doug Mackay picked up the ball and placed it on the spot. He had been taking Bromfield's penalties since his arrival, and boasted a 100 per cent scoring record thus far. In the radio and television booths, however, breathless commentators compelled listeners and viewers to cast their minds back six months, to the fateful moment that had effectively began Doug's exile from the Premier League. Would he, could he miss another penalty of even greater magnitude and value? Was he himself in a state of panic as he prepared for what might prove to be the defining moment of his career? Or was he about to come full circle and write the greatest moment in Bromfield's history?

The scene was set, the cameras poised and the inconceivable circumstances acknowledged as Doug stepped back from the ball.

In the stands, Ally, Ryan and Doug's parents were mere specks among the multitude. He blotted out images of past failures as he braced himself for the referee's signal. This was no time to think, no time to philosophise.

There was just him, a ball, a goalkeeper and twelve yards between them. The shrill sound of the referee's whistle cut through the humid afternoon air and Doug sprang forward, the conviction that the glory of his future rested neither on penalties scored or missed, but on the hope he had in God.

Then he watched, as if in slow motion, as the perfectly struck ball sailed with surgical precision straight into the top right-hand corner of the net.

CHRISTIAN FOCUS PUBLICATIONS

Christian Focus · Christian Heritage · CF4K · Mentor

Christian Focus Publications publishes books for adults and children under its four main imprints: Christian Focus, Christian Heritage, CF4K and Mentor. Our books reflect that God's word is reliable and Jesus is the way to know him, and live for ever with him.

Our children's publication list includes a Sunday school curriculum that covers pre-school to early teens; puzzle and activity books. We also publish personal and family devotional titles, biographies and inspirational stories that children will love.

If you are looking for quality Bible teaching for children then we have an excellent range of Bible story and age specific theological books.

From pre-school to teenage fiction, we have it covered!

Find us at our web page:
www.christianfocus.com

CF4•K
Because you're never
too young to know Jesus